The Waiting Game . . .

Clint grabbed a straight-backed wooden chair from the hotel lobby, took it outside with him, and sat. They were going to have to come after him, or take the chance he would expose them. He wasn't doing this for Joe Hickey. Hickey was going to get his neck stretched eventually . . .

This was for whoever had sent him that message on the wind . . .

He saw them now, walking down the street, carrying shotguns. Four scatterguns could do a lot of damage, and some of that would be accidental.

He remained seated and calm as they approached. He hoped that steady nerves would be on his side.

THE GUNSMITH

334

MESSAGE ON THE WIND

J. R. ROBERTS

JOVE BOOKS, NEW YORK

THE BERKLEY PUBLISHING GROUP
Published by the Penguin Group
Penguin Group (USA) Inc.
375 Hudson Street, New York, New York 10014, USA
Penguin Group (Canada), 90 Eglinton Avenue East, Suite 700, Toronto, Ontario M4P 2Y3, Canada
(a division of Pearson Penguin Canada Inc.)
Penguin Books Ltd., 80 Strand, London WC2R 0RL, England
Penguin Group Ireland, 25 St. Stephen's Green, Dublin 2, Ireland (a division of Penguin Books Ltd.)
Penguin Group (Australia), 250 Camberwell Road, Camberwell, Victoria 3124, Australia
(a division of Pearson Australia Group Pty. Ltd.)
Penguin Books India Pvt. Ltd., 11 Community Centre, Panchsheel Park, New Delhi—110 017, India
Penguin Group (NZ), 67 Apollo Drive, Rosedale, North Shore 0632, New Zealand
(a division of Pearson New Zealand Ltd.)
Penguin Books (South Africa) (Pty.) Ltd., 24 Sturdee Avenue, Rosebank, Johannesburg 2196,
South Africa

Penguin Books Ltd., Registered Offices: 80 Strand, London WC2R 0RL, England

This is a work of fiction. Names, characters, places, and incidents either are the product of the author's imagination or are used fictitiously, and any resemblance to actual persons, living or dead, business establishments, events, or locales is entirely coincidental.

MESSAGE ON THE WIND

A Jove Book / published by arrangement with the author

PRINTING HISTORY
Jove edition / October 2009

Copyright © 2009 by Robert J. Randisi.
Cover illustration by Sergio Giovine.

ISBN: 978-0-515-14727-8

JOVE®
Jove Books are published by The Berkley Publishing Group,
a division of Penguin Group (USA) Inc.,
375 Hudson Street, New York, New York 10014.
JOVE® is a registered trademark of Penguin Group (USA) Inc.
The "J" design is a trademark of Penguin Group (USA) Inc.

PRINTED IN THE UNITED STATES OF AMERICA

10 9 8 7 6 5 4 3 2 1

ONE

The wind carries many things.

The smells of bacon and coffee, to give away the location of a campfire.

The sound of horses' hooves, giving away the presence of approaching rider or riders.

The sound of voices, giving away the contents of a conversation.

The smell of fear.

The Gunsmith had experienced all of these, but he was about to experience something brand-new . . .

The wind was arid, far from a respite from the Arizona heat. It was strong, though, whipping up sand and debris, so Clint thought it wise to make camp and wait it out. If he could find some sort of shelter, it would save his eyes and the eyes of his Darley Arabian, Eclipse. Luckily, he found a rock formation that afforded them some shelter, although he still needed to cover both their heads with a blanket.

He stood next to the horse for hours, sharing the blanket that was shielding not only their eyes but their hides from the biting sand. When the wind died down sufficiently, he was able to remove the blanket, unsaddle Eclipse, and then sit and rest his legs. Finally, the wind died down enough so that he could build a fire and make some coffee.

As he sat and ate a meal of coffee and beef jerky, the wind became a breeze, the kind that whistled softly in his ears.

As it started to get dark, he went about making their shelter comfortable for the night. He had nothing to feed Eclipse, but he gave him some water. Then he laid out his bedroll and fed the fire enough wood to keep it going. He rolled himself in his blanket, set his gun belt by his head, and went to sleep. It wasn't late, but there was nothing else to do.

He woke twice during the night, just as the fire was dying down. He stoked it both times, and went back to sleep. The next time he woke it was morning. The sun was shining, the breeze was still blowing, and something was on his face.

He reached up quickly and grabbed it, worried it might be a scorpion or tarantula. As it turned out, it was a piece of paper. He crumpled it and, for some reason, shoved it into his pocket.

He made a fresh pot of coffee, and once again made a meal of beef jerky. He had a can of peaches left, but he was saving it. Coffee and jerky were usually his staples, though, enabling him to travel light.

He watered Eclipse again, then saddled him and broke camp, kicking the fire to death and stowing his blanket and bedroll. He mounted up and rode out of the shelter. He hadn't seen a signpost for some time, but he believed he was approaching a town. The path he was riding was not a road, but it was much traveled, nevertheless. That led him to believe it would lead him to a town. He'd ridden through Arizona before, but he was not familiar with this section of southern Arizona. If he were nearer the border of Mexico, he could have stopped in Tombstone, or even Bisbee. Farther northwest he could have headed to Tucson. And farther east he could have made his way to Yuma. But in this particular section of southern Arizona he wasn't sure what town he was heading for.

If he continued to ride south, he'd eventually end up in Mexico. But he hoped to come to a town before then.

As he continued on, he reached into his pocket for the piece of paper that had blown onto his face that morning. Pulling it out, he uncrumpled it and smoothed it out. It appeared to be a piece torn from a newspaper, but there was something written on it. The handwriting was a scrawl, which could have been a child's, or an adult's under stress. He held it up to the sun in an attempt to read it. There seemed to be three words written in pencil. It said: *Please help us.*

He turned the paper over and found that it had been torn from the top of a newspaper page. Therefore, the name of the newspaper was legible. It was called the

Organ Pipe Register. However, the name of the state
was missing. Organ Pipe . . . where? Clint thought.

But also legible was the date: April 11 . . . two years
ago!

TWO

Clint had heard stories about the early settlers, traveling by wagon train, who used to leave notes on the road for those coming after them. Some of the notes were for family, to tell them which way to come. Others were left for anyone coming after, strangers, warning them about what direction not to take. They were left hanging on tree branches, under rocks, and more often than not a wind would blow them away and they would never get to the ones they were intended for.

Clint was holding a note that appeared to have been written two years ago. He had no way of knowing if it had ever reached its intended reader. Also, he didn't know what state the town of Organ Pipe was in. Chances were it was Arizona; otherwise this note had been blown from one state to another, and maybe more.

He folded the note and put it in his shirt pocket. When he got to the next town he'd ask about Organ

Pipe. At the moment that was his goal: get to the next town.

When he came within sight of the town an hour later, he realized that the word "town" just barely applied. He could count the buildings from where he was. Six. One of them was large enough to be a hotel. The others varied in size, and one appeared to be a livery stable. A hotel, a stable, and some food—that's what he needed. And a cold beer.

He rode down the hill and onto the road that led into town. It seemed to be the only street the town had.

As he rode in, he didn't see any people on the street. Some of the buildings had their doors open, including the large one. Nailed above the door was a crudely handwritten sign that said "HOTEL–SALOON–RESTAURANT." A little bit of everything, Clint thought. Across the street a building one third the size of the hotel had another crudely written sign that said "SHERIFF–UNDERTAKER." Now, that would be an unusual man.

He reined in Eclipse in front of the big building and dismounted.

"Be patient, big fella," he said, patting the horse's massive neck. "I'll get you fed as soon as I can."

He stepped up onto the boardwalk and through the batwing doors. Three men turned and looked at him, including the bartender.

"Welcome, stranger," he said, smiling. "Stiff wind blow you our way?"

"It sure did," Clint said, approaching the bar. One of the other men was leaning on it, while the third man was sitting at a table alone with a bottle of whiskey and a glass.

"Mind telling me where I am?" Clint asked.

"Sure," the bartender said. "This is Miller's Crossing. It ain't much, but it's home to twenty-two of us. Get ya somethin'?"

"A beer?"

"Comin' up."

In a second the bartender put a frothy mug in front of Clint.

"'Fraid it ain't cold, but it's wet."

"I'll settle for wet, right now," Clint said. He took a couple of gulps, almost gagged, and put the glass down.

"Yeah, I know," the barman said. "Hard to take. That's why most of the folks hereabouts drink whiskey."

"I need a room, a meal, and board for my horse. Can I get all that here in Miller's Crossing?"

"Sure can," the man said. "We got all the comforts of home."

"Who do I see?"

"Well, me for the meal and room, and Antoine down to the livery stable. You wanna take your horse down there? I'll have the meal ready when you get back. You mind beans?"

"Beans and what?"

"Beans and beans right now," the man said. "It's all we got. Might find a hunk of bacon around that I can cut into it."

"That'll do."

"I'm Benny," the man said. "Benny the Bull, they call me, 'cause I'm so big."

Clint studied the man and found him to be about six-two, just slightly taller than he was.

"Yeah, I know," Benny said, "I ain't so big, but I'm the biggest man in town. Anyway, tell Antoine I sent ya, and not to overcharge ya because you're a stranger."

"Okay," Clint said, "I'll tell him. Thanks."

"When ya get back, I'll give ya the best room in the house," Benny called after him as he went out the door. "The Presidential Suite!"

THREE

When he got to the livery, Clint found that Antoine was a black man with a distinct New Orleans accent. He told the man Benny sent him, but that didn't matter. As soon as he saw Eclipse, Antoine got a big grin on his face.

"Dat's some horse, Boss," he said to Clint. "I gon' take good care of this horse, me."

"How did you get from New Orleans to here, Antoine?" Clint asked.

"Don' ask, Boss," Antoine said. "It ain't a pretty story."

Clint was satisfied that the man would take good care of Eclipse, so he didn't press him for his story. He paid him in advance for a day, then asked, "Have you ever heard of a town called Organ Pipe?"

Antoine's face changed, losing his smile.

"Why you askin' dat, Boss?" he asked.

"Just a name I came across lately, and I'd never heard of it."

"Dat ain't no place you wan' go," Antoine said. "I'd never go there, me."

"Why not?"

"Dat a bad place, Boss," Antoine said.

"Do you know where it is?"

"Don' know, don' wan' know," Antoine said, shaking his head.

"Well, is it in Arizona?"

"You ask somebody else, Boss," Antoine said. "I take care of your horse."

"Okay, Antoine," he said. "I'll ask somebody else."

"You do dat, Boss."

Antoine walked Eclipse to the back of the stable as Clint left.

When he got back to the saloon-hotel-restaurant, Benny the Bull had a steaming plate of beans waiting on the bar for him. As Clint got closer, he could smell the bacon. Apparently, Benny had found that hunk he'd been talking about.

"Found that bacon," Benny said. "Had a little green on it, but I sliced it off. The rest seemed okay."

"I'm hungry enough to try it."

"Ain't got no fork, but I give ya a spoon."

"I'll make do."

"Want a beer with that?"

"How about a whiskey?" Clint didn't usually drink whiskey, but he didn't think he could stomach another of Benny the Bull's beers.

"Comin' up."

There were still only two other men in the saloon,

and neither had said a word the whole time Clint was there.

"I'll bet you're passin' through," Benny said.

"That'd be a good bet."

"On the way to where?"

Clint almost said "Nowhere" but instead he said, "Organ Pipe."

"Where?"

"A town called Organ Pipe."

"I never heard of that," Benny said. He looked over at the other two men. "Ever heard of a town called Organ Pipe?"

The two men shook their heads and looked away. Clint had a feeling all three men were lying.

"Guess I'll have to ask somebody else where it is," he said.

"You don't know?"

"No," Clint said, "I just ran across the name recently, sounded interesting."

"Sounds odd to me," Benny said, "but can't say I'd be interested enough to go lookin'."

"I wander, anyway," Clint said. "Just thought I'd try to find it. Think anyone else in town's ever heard of it?"

"Can't say," Benny said.

"Maybe I'll ask the sheriff," Clint said. "Or the undertaker. Oh, wait, they're the same guy. That's kind of odd, ain't it?"

"Wait until you meet him," Benny said. "Then you'll find out what odd is."

Clint scooped some beans into his mouth.

"I'll go and see him when I finish eating," he said. "Can I get a glass of water?"

"Sure. Lukewarm okay?"

"Lukewarm's fine."

Benny went to get the water.

After he finished eating, washing it down with brackish water that was at least better than the warm beer, Clint left the saloon and crossed the street to the office of the sheriff-undertaker. He didn't say good-bye to Benny, who must have been in the back room when he left. He still had to get his room, so he'd go back right after his conversation with the law.

He entered the sheriff's office. It had a lot of the conventions of the office—desk, potbellied stove, gun rack—but it also had some of the look of an undertaker's office. There were even some coffins stacked over on one side. There was a curtained doorway that could have led to a cell block, or an undertaker's back room. There could have been bodies back there right at that moment—alive or dead.

"Hello?" Clint called.

"Be right out," someone yelled from the back room.

Clint noticed the musty smell of the place, as if it hadn't been used in a while. There was a layer of dust on the desk. Maybe no one had died or been arrested in Miller's Crossing in a long time.

Finally, the curtains of the doorway were swept aside and a man walked in.

"Benny?" Clint asked.

"Benny the Bull, sheriff and undertaker of Miller's Crossing, at your service," the man said, with a smile.

"You hold these jobs, too?"

"You bet," he said. "I pretty much run everything here."

"Where's your badge?"

"Oh, I keep it here in a drawer. I don't wear it unless I need it."

"And what do the other twenty-one people in town do?"

"Well, you met Antoine, he owns the livery," Benny said. "And he has a daughter. The rest of the citizens pretty much do what those fellas over in the saloon are doin' now. They just sit, and wait."

"For what?"

"Who knows?"

"And you still don't know anything about a town called Organ Pipe?"

"I told you in the saloon, mister . . . Hey, you never told me your name."

"My name is Clint Adams."

"Clint . . . Adams?"

"That's right."

"Um, well, I got your room ready, Mr. Adams, if you want to go over there and see it now."

Clint had been toting his saddlebags and rifle with him since leaving his horse at the livery.

"That's a good idea, Benny," he said, "or should I call you Sheriff?"

"Naw, Benny'll do just fine, Mr. Adams," the man said, nervously. "This way."

FOUR

The hotel room was a lot like the sheriff's office—stuffy and dusty. Clint told Benny it was fine, and then when the man left, he opened the window to air it out.

Miller's Crossing was two things—a dying town and one man's kingdom. Obviously folks had left little by little, and probably still were leaving. Clint wondered what Benny would do when the last of the other twenty-one people left town.

But there were eighteen other people in town who Clint had not asked about Organ Pipe, so he decided to go out and take a walk around.

There were shops in town. Whenever Clint entered one, he wouldn't have been surprised to see Benny the Bull behind the counter, but it didn't happen. Apparently, he confined his time to being sheriff and undertaker, and running the saloon-restaurant-hotel.

Clint talked to the clerks in a hardware store, a small

barely stocked general store, and a barbershop. He asked them about a town called Organ Pipe and they all did the same thing.

They lied.

By the time Clint got back to his hotel room, he was convinced of one thing. Organ Pipe was in Arizona, and it was probably somewhere in the area. Otherwise why would everyone in this dying town have some reason to lie about it?

There were sections of Arizona he knew well, so Organ Pipe had to be in this area, which he did not know well. Or maybe it *had* been in this area but was gone now. Maybe, like Miller's Crossing, it had dwindled down until, finally, the last person left and the town just died.

But the note that had fluttered over his face had been written on a piece of newspaper that had been published two years ago. That meant that, at the very least, the town of Organ Pipe had still been around two years ago.

Still, riding out and going in circles until he found Organ Pipe was not the way to go. He needed to find somebody who knew something.

One of these people had to talk to him.

"Is there some other place to eat besides here?" Clint asked Benny when he came back down from his room.

"There are some homes where cookin' is done," Benny said. "Wives for husbands, daughters for fathers, but for the public? I'm afraid this is the only place."

"And all you have is beans?"

"Yeah," Benny said, "and no more bacon to put in it."

"I guess I should spend the night, then, and move on," Clint said.

"That's what everyone does," Benny said. "I mean, we don't get many people here, but when they do come, some don't even stop; others spend one night and go."

"Okay," Clint said, "thanks."

As he started to leave, Benny called, "Will you be back to eat?"

"Probably," Clint said. "I mean, what other choice do I have?"

As Clint left, Benny took his shotgun out from beneath the bar and checked it.

FIVE

For want of something better to do, Clint went to the livery stable to check on Eclipse. As Clint entered, he heard someone talking in very low tones, almost cooing. Most of the stalls were empty, but when he got to the back, he saw Eclipse. In the stall with him was a girl who was stroking his neck, talking to him softly.

"Hello," Clint said.

The girl's head swiveled around at the sound of his voice, her eyes wide.

"Goddamn, you scared me!"

"Sorry," he said, "I didn't mean to."

"What do you want?"

She was black, young, and pretty. He assumed she was Antoine's daughter. While she stared at him, she continued to stroke Eclipse's neck, and the big black Darley Arabian seemed to be enjoying it.

"I've never seen him take to anyone this quickly before," he said to her.

Her face brightened. "Is he yours?"

"Yes."

"Does he have a name?"

"Eclipse."

"Eclipse," she repeated, then looked at the horse and said, "Hey, Eclipse? How ya doin', boy?"

"And what's your name?" Clint asked.

"I'm Jada," she said. "This is the most magnificent horse I've ever seen."

"You should've seen Duke," Clint said. "A big black gelding, no white on him at all. Just midnight black and huge."

"Bigger than Eclipse?"

"Seventeen hands, if he was an inch."

"What happened to him?"

"What happens to us all," Clint said. "He got old and I had to put him out to pasture. That's when I got Eclipse."

"That's amazing," she said. "How did you come to have two such magnificent horses?"

"Both were gifts, from men I knew," Clint said. He didn't bother to tell her it was Jesse James who made him a gift of Duke, or that P. T. Barnum had given him Eclipse. She might not have believed either story.

"Who?"

"Just friends."

"You have good friends," she said. "But you just left him with us today. Why are you back?"

"Just to check up on him."

"Antoine will take good care of him," she said. "I'll help."

"Antoine," Clint said, "is he your . . ."

"Husband," she said, before Clint could say, "Father." "He's very good with horses."

Clint thought Antoine had to be thirty years older than she was, but he had seen oddly coupled people before.

"Well, there's not much to do in this town," he said. "I just thought I'd come and stay with this old boy for a while. Besides, all I've got to look forward to back at the saloon is more beans, and without bacon this time."

"There is nowhere else to eat around here," she agreed, "unless, of course, you happen to know somebody who can cook."

"I'm afraid I don't know anyone," he told her.

"Well," she said, turning to face him, "you know me, and I can cook."

"Antoine—"

"He wouldn't mind," she said. "You're a customer, and a stranger. He won't mind that I've invited you for supper."

"You have?"

"Yes, I have. Will you accept?"

"Well," he said, "since you're taking such good care of Eclipse, how can I refuse?"

SIX

On the way to the house Jada asked, "What's your name, mister?"

"Clint," he said, deliberately leaving his last name out of the conversation, for the moment.

"Well, Clint, I'm makin' fried chicken and some greens. Does that sound okay?"

"It sounds fine, but . . . where do you get it?"

"Ain't really chicken, it's these prairie chickens. I go out and catch them."

"You hunt them?"

"Yeah, but not with a gun," she said. "Ain't no fun digging lead out of a cooked chicken. Uh-uh, I catch 'em and wring their necks. I'm fast."

Clint believed that Jada was fast. She was whipcord thin, not very tall, with a slim waist and hard breasts, like ripe peaches. Her hair was short and black, and she apparently kept it clean. In fact, he could smell the soap she used when she washed.

The house wasn't very far from the livery. When they reached it, Clint saw that it was little more than a shack. Someone had done work on it, though, to make it sturdy. Probably Antoine.

As Jada opened the door to let them in, Antoine shouted, "Where you been, gal? I'm hungry."

"We got company, Antoine," she said.

"Company?" He had been facing the fireplace. Now he turned, and when he saw Clint he froze.

"This is the feller who owns that big black," she said. "His name's Clint. I invited him to supper so he don't have ta eat Benny's beans."

"I know who he is," Antoine said. "I been takin' good care of your horse, Boss."

"I know you have, Antoine," Clint said. "If this is a problem, Antoine, I can leave—"

"Naw, ya ain't got ta leave, Boss," Antoine said. "Da gal invited ya, ya gots to stay. You set, I'm gon' get some more wood for the fire, me."

"I'll get supper goin'," Jada said.

They went to do their chores, leaving Clint standing in front of the fireplace alone. He didn't know what to do, but the thought of fried chicken kept him there.

Antoine returned with the wood, set it down by the fireplace, and added a few pieces to the fire.

"Set yerself down," he said. "We gots two chairs."

"But, Jada—"

"She don't need ta set," Antoine said. "She's young. Besides, she gon' be cookin'."

The chairs were wooden, made by hand, with cushions that also looked homemade. Chairs by Antoine, cushions by Jada, he was sure.

"You've made this place nice and sturdy, Antoine," Clint said.

"I'm good wit' my hands, Boss," Antoine said. "This ol' shack was fallin' down, but I fixed it up, me."

Clint turned his head, looked at the table they were going to eat on.

"Made this chair and that table, too," Antoine said. "I's good wit' wood, and wit' horses, me."

"Well," Clint said, "if you're as good with horses as you are around here, I can see I've got no reason to worry about Eclipse."

"You wan' a drink, boss? I got some whiskey I picks up when I go to town."

"Town?"

Antoine got up and reached into a wooden chest to pull out a bottle of whiskey. He looked very happy as he went to the kitchen to fetch a couple of mismatched glasses.

"You take it easy on that whiskey, Pops," Jada scolded him.

"Dat's what we say when we goes to Yuma," Antoine explained, as he poured whiskey into the two glasses and handed Clint one. "Town. Dat's where we pick up most of our supplies."

"You and Jada?"

"All of us, Boss," Antoine said. "All of us dat lives here in Miller's Crossing."

"So . . . you all go?"

"No," Antoine said, "A few of us goes there every month. We draw straws to see who goes, so the same people don't always do it. It's about a six-day ride, dere and back."

"I love when it's our turn to go to Yuma," Jada said, turning from the stove to face them. She had put on a small apron. "I get to dress up, and we eat in a restaurant, stay in a hotel."

"Hush up, girl," Antoine said. "You jes' keep cookin'."

"Don't you worry, Pops," she said, laughing. "Your supper's gonna be good. I caught three nice fat birds this morning and I'm gonna cook 'em all."

To Clint, that sounded just fine.

SEVEN

The fried prairie chicken was excellent, the best meal Clint had had in weeks. He and Antoine finished off the whiskey bottle during the meal, and only the fact that they had been eating while drinking kept them from being completely drunk.

Toward the end of the meal Antoine was drunk enough, though, to let Jada have a couple of nips from the bottle, as well. By the end of the meal they were all full and happy, laughing together until Clint asked a question he'd been saving.

"Since you travel fairly often," Clint asked, "I figure one of you must know where this town called Organ Pipe is."

Antoine and Jada stared at him, the laughter dying in Antoine's eyes. Jada wasn't sure what had just happened, but she knew her husband wasn't happy anymore.

"Why you keep on ast dat, Boss?" he asked Clint.

"Like I said, it's just a name I've heard," Clint said. "I don't have anyplace in particular to go, so I thought I'd take a look. You have to admit, it's an unusual name for a town."

"It is kinda unusual, yeah," Antoine said.

"So?" Clint asked. "You know where it is then?"

"No," Antoine said, "I ain't got no idea." He stood up. "I got to go back to the stable and bed down the horses. You stay here, Boss. Jada give you some beaucoup coffee."

"That sounds good to me, if Jada doesn't mind."

"I don't mind," she said. "I'll clear up and make it right away."

"I be back later," Antoine said.

"If I'm not here when you get back," Clint said, "thank you for the meal."

"You thank Jada," Antoine said. "She da one dat cook you dat meal, Boss."

Antoine left, and Clint remained seated while Jada cleaned up and made coffee.

"I didn't have time to make no pie," she apologized.

"That's okay," Clint said. "That was a great meal, and this is really good coffee."

"I'm real glad you liked it all."

She sat across from him, drinking her coffee while holding the cup in both hands. In watching her move around the kitchen, Clint had realized she was not as thin as he had first thought. She was wearing jeans and filled them out nicely, with a very solid butt to go with her hard breasts. She also had a pouty mouth that she seemed to constantly be wetting with her tongue. If it wasn't for the fact that she was married to Antoine, Clint would have been trying to have her as his dessert.

"What you lookin' at?" she asked him.

"Hmm? Oh, nothin'—"

"You was lookin' at me."

"Well, you're very pretty, Jada."

"You think so?"

"Come on," he said, "you know so."

"How would I know that?" she asked. "Ain't nobody in this town tells me that."

"Well, you're married to Antoine," Clint said.

"Oh, he don't never tell me."

"Other men would probably tell you, but it looks to me like after Benny, it's Antoine who's the biggest man in town."

"He big and strong, all right," Jada said, "but he's no damn good when it comes to treatin' a woman right."

"Then why did you marry him?" Clint asked.

She bit her lip, which somehow made his mouth water.

"If I tell you somethin', you promise not to tell anybody else?"

"Sure, Jada," he said, "you can tell me anything."

"We ain't really married."

"What?"

"Antoine bought me from my daddy in New Orleans, and then brought me here to keep house for him and be his wife. Only we ain't never got married."

"Why not?"

"Well, for one thing there ain't no preacher here," she explained.

"And what about when you go to Yuma?"

"Then we're too busy to do it," she said.

"So you just won't ever do it?"

"I don't know," she said with a shrug. "He don't seem to care, and I sure don't. In fact, I'd rather not be married to him."

"Why not?"

"'Cause then I can leave anytime I want to," she said. "Or do anythin' I want to."

"Like what?"

"Like slippin' off your britches and sexin' you down," she said.

He rocked back in his chair. He'd never quite heard it put like that before.

EIGHT

Jada got up and moved around to Clint's side of the table.

"You ain't got to worry about Antoine," she told him. "He's gonna be at the stable for a while."

"He doesn't have that many horses," Clint warned.

"He's gonna make sure your horse is well taken care of, and then he's gonna put out a bottle of whiskey he don't know I know he hides there. He won't be back for hours."

She got on her knees in front of Clint who, in spite of himself, had turned to face her. Her fingers plucked at his gun belt, and his pants belt, so she could open his pants and stick her hand inside.

"Oooh," she said, as she closed her hand around his hardness.

"Jada—"

She squeezed him lovingly and then pulled his hard cock out into the light.

"I knew when I saw you, and you said you was the owner of that beautiful horse, I just knew . . ."

"Knew what?"

"That you would be a special man," she said, "and you are."

She opened those pouty lips and slid his penis into her mouth, began to suck him wetly, moaning all the while.

"Oh yes," she said, letting his wet penis slide free. "Antoine hardly ever gets hard anymore. It's been a long time for me . . ."

She took him in her mouth again, at the same time yanking on his pants to get them down. He had to lift his butt off the chair so she could slide his trousers and underwear down to his ankles. His gun belt was on the floor next to him where he could reach it, but he was still worried that Antoine would come back while his pants were down around his ankles, putting him at a disadvantage.

But Jada didn't give him time to think about that. She quickly got to her feet and kicked off her boots, peeled off all her clothes until she was naked. Her skin was dark, but her nipples were darker still. The hair between her legs was as black as it could be.

She leaped into his lap, pressing her breasts against his face. He opened his mouth to take her nipples in and suck them. They were hard, and as big as juicy berries. She rubbed her wet pussy against his hard cock as she kissed him, driving her tongue into his mouth and groaning deep in her throat. Finally, she lifted her hips and came down on him, taking him into her wet, steamy depths.

Her breath caught in her throat and she made a sound that, at first, made him think she was choking. He soon found that she would make this sound periodically during their coupling. It was a high-pitched gasp, a sound she made in between words, as she talked while she was bouncing up and down on his rigid cock.

"Oooh, yeah," she said, "God . . . damn . . . yeah . . . oooh . . . oh . . . oooh . . ."

"Oooh," was a major part of her vocabulary during sex, apparently. She'd catch her breath, and then say "Oooh" several times in a row, then catch her breath again with that high-pitched noise, then breathe noisily between her teeth as she rode him.

Clint had her ass in his hands, feeling her wetness there, making her slick to hold. So he stood and deposited her on the table, grabbed her ankles and spread her so he could fuck her hard and fast. On some level he realized his back was now to the door and if Antoine came in he was vulnerable—but he soon forgot about that and would only kick himself about it later.

He was fascinated by Jada's face, which in the throes of passion became incredibly beautiful. Her lips seemed to swell and become even fuller, and when she bit them he almost expected them to yield juice, like ripe fruit. Her nostrils flared as she breathed raggedly. Her breasts were larger than he'd thought while she was dressed, her nipples swollen.

He held her by the hips and drove into her, testing the

resolve of the table beneath her. It wiggled and leaped and moved across the floor as he fucked her.

And she got loud.

And louder.

He wondered how far away she could be heard. As far away as the stable?

He began to fuck her faster and faster, and she began to shout to him to go faster, and harder, and don't stop.

Clint's own breath began coming in rasps, though nothing as sexy as that high-pitched sound Jada was still making.

He finally decided that this had to come to an end for both of them, in case Antoine came back. He wasn't really looking forward to killing his host.

As he felt her begin to tremble, he felt his own release coming to a boil and knew that this was going to be close, very, very close . . .

He hoped the table could take it.

NINE

Clint got dressed, said good-bye to Jada, and got away from there before Antoine could return. All the way back to town he was kicking himself for making himself so vulnerable. A great meal and a beautiful woman were nothing to die over—or to kill for. If Antoine had returned there would have been trouble, whether Jada was really married to him or not.

It was dark by the time he reached the hotel. He considered going up to his room, but decided to see if any other citizens of Miller's Crossing were in the saloon.

When he got in there, he saw the bartender behind the bar and three other people—only one more than before. He studied the three of them, but couldn't really tell if two of them were the same two from before.

At the bar he suddenly got the urge for a cold beer. Maybe none of these people could tell him where Organ Pipe was, but they could certainly tell him where he could find a cold beer.

"Just head for Yuma," the bartender told him. "You'll come to a town called Rosewood. They got two saloons, and both serve cold beer."

"I guess I should do that tomorrow," Clint said. "It's been a while since I had a cold beer."

"They got a whorehouse and a sheriff, too," Benny said, "so ya better watch yerself while yer there."

"I always watch myself, Benny," Clint said.

"Sure ya don't wanna stay awhile?"

"Why would I want to stay?" Clint asked.

Benny shrugged.

"Do me some good," he said to Clint. "Yer my only cash customer."

"Well," Clint said, "I'm sorry about that, but I think I've got to be moving on."

"Still lookin' for that town?" Benny asked. "What was it? Lead Pipe?"

"Organ Pipe."

"Oh, yeah," Benny said, "that's right."

"Still never heard of it?"

"Ain't nothin' happened to change it," Benny said.

"I was just wondering," Clint said. "Folks around here seem to get nervous when I mention it."

"Nervous?"

"Yup."

"Don't know what they'd have to be nervous about."

"Neither do I," Clint said. "All I'm doing is looking for a town."

"Well, there's plenty of towns in all directions from here," Benny said. "Like I said, Rosewood ain't too far, probably just a day's ride."

If it had been a few hours earlier, Clint would have left and taken advantage of remaining daylight, but that wasn't the case. He was kind of worried about Jada and Antoine, and what would happen if the man came home and realized his wife had had sex with him.

"Tell me something," he said to Benny.

"If I can."

"Antoine and his woman Jada," Clint said. "Are they married?"

"Well," Benny said, leaning on the bar and lowering his voice, "they're supposed ta be, as far as anybody knows, but Antoine got drunk in here one night and told me he ain't married to her. He just bought her from her daddy."

"You mean . . . like a slave?"

"I s'pose," Benny said. "I don't much like to think of it that way."

"Neither do I."

"But she don't seem ta wanna run away none."

Clint nodded his agreement.

"She sure is a sweet-lookin' little thing, though," Benny said. "But that Antoine, he's big and he can be mean."

"But you're bigger," Clint observed.

"Don't think I'm meaner, though," Benny said. "I mean, I'm pretty easygoin'."

"Is that a fact?"

Benny grinned.

"Long as ya don't get me mad."

"I'll try not to do that, the rest of the time I'm here," Clint promised.

As Clint pushed away from the bar, Benny asked, "Headin' back to your room?"

"Might as well."

"Ya wouldn't be wantin' a woman for the night, wouldja?"

"I don't think so, Benny," Clint said.

"Be better than the beer, I guarantee ya."

"It would have to be," Clint said, "but I'll just pass. Thanks."

"Suit yerself."

Clint nodded and went up to his room.

TEN

Clint was sitting up in his bed, reading, when there was a knock on the door. In fact, it was more than a knock, it was a pounding. That meant it was probably a man, and an agitated one. Clint was afraid he knew what man in town he had caused some agitation.

He grabbed his gun from his holster hanging on the bedpost and walked to the door.

"Who is it?" he asked.

"It's Antoine, Boss. Lemme in!"

"It's late, Antoine—" Clint said.

The man started pounding on the door again, demanding to be let in. He sounded drunk. Clint decided he had to let him in or he'd attract attention from downstairs—if there was anyone in the saloon at that moment.

"Okay, Antoine, okay," Clint said. He opened the door and backed away, holding his gun behind him.

The big black man came staggering in, as if he'd

been leaning on the door. He righted himself, then squinted owlishly at Clint.

"We gots ta close the do'," he said. He put his finger to his lips and shut the door.

"What's going on, Antoine?" Clint asked.

Antoine brought his hand up. Clint flinched for a moment, until he saw that the man was holding a mostly empty whiskey bottle.

"Ya wants a drink, Boss?"

"No, thanks, Antoine."

Clint walked to the bed and holstered the gun, then turned to face the drunk black man. Antoine wasn't acting as if he knew anything about Clint and Jada.

"It's late, Antoine," he said. "What's on your mind?"

"It ain't dat late, Boss," Antoine said. "We could go downstairs and gets another bottle."

"I don't think so. Why don't you just finish that one all by yourself?"

"Don't mind if I do." He raised the bottle and drank down the rest of the whiskey. He staggered, and for a moment Clint thought he was going to fall, but then he righted himself and grinned. "Done!"

"And time for you to go home," Clint said. "I'm sure your wife is worried about you."

"Ah, she ain't worried," Antoine said. "And just between you an' me, she ain't really my wife."

"What?"

"I bought her from her daddy in New Orleans and brought her here wit' me. So believe me, she ain't gon' be worried about me."

"Antoine, come on—"

"Besides," the older black man said, with a wink, "I got somethin' important to talk ta you about."

"And what's that?"

"I gots ta sit down," Antoine said. "The room is sorta . . . spinnin'."

"Here." Clint got Antoine to a straight-backed chair against the wall before the man could sit on his bed.

"Thank you, Boss."

Antoine sank heavily onto the chair, leaning his head against the wall.

"Antoine," Clint said, "what is it you have to talk to me about?"

"Place," the old black man mumbled.

"What place?"

"Place . . . you . . . asked about . . ." His head tilted forward until his chin rested on his chest.

"Antoine! Hey!" Clint snapped, grabbing the man's shoulders and shaking him. "What place? You mean Organ Pipe?"

Antoine's eyes snapped open and he stared at Clint.

"Whatchoo doin'?" he demanded.

"Antoine, come on. What were you going to tell me?" Clint asked.

"About what?" The man squinted, looking around. "Where am I, Boss? I s'posed to be home."

"Antoine, you're in my hotel room."

"How I got here?"

"You came on your own. You said you had something to tell me."

"I gots ta get home, Boss," Antoine said. He tried to get up, but couldn't, no matter how much he struggled.

"All right, all right," Clint said. "Let me get my boots on and I'll take you home."

"Thanks, Boss," Antoine said. "Jada gon' be awful mad at me."

"Well," Clint said, pulling on his boots, "let's see how quick we can get you home, then."

Clint grabbed Antoine's hand and pulled him to his feet.

"Thank ya much, Boss."

ELEVEN

When they pushed open the door to Antoine and Jada's shack, the girl looked at them in surprise. Antoine was leaning on Clint, who was having trouble holding the large man's weight.

"What happened?" she asked.

"He came to my room drunk," Clint said, "and couldn't get back here on his own."

Jada came over to take Antoine from Clint.

"I'll put him to bed."

"Can you handle it?" he asked. "Do you need help?"

"No," she said, "I've done it before. Please, you just wait here."

She got Antoine into the other room with remarkable ease. Through the door Clint could see that there was just barely enough room for a bed in there. She dropped him onto it, then came out and closed the door behind her. She approached Clint with a lascivious smile on her face and cupped his crotch.

"You came back for more already?" she asked.

"Jada, no," Clint said, swatting her hand away. "Not with Antoine in the next room."

"He won't hear a thing," she assured him. "He'll sleep like the dead till mornin'."

"I need to talk to you," he said, moving away from her. She had a powerful sexual presence that had his cock already hard, but he was determined not to give in. Not this time.

"Talk? About what?"

"Before he passed out," Clint said, "Antoine said he had something to tell me."

"What?"

"I couldn't get it out of him," he said, "but he mentioned the place I was asking about."

"What place?"

"You remember," he said. "I asked you both about a place called Organ Pipe. You both lied to me and said you'd never heard of it."

"Organ Pipe?" she repeated. "I never have."

"Well, maybe you haven't, but I'm willing to bet Antoine and probably the longtime residents of this town have."

She shrugged.

"I don't know," she said. "I can't tell you anythin' about that."

"I want to talk to Antoine in the morning," he said. "I want to find out what he knows. I'll need your help."

"If you want my help," she said, "you will have to do somethin' for me."

"Jada, I said not here," he said.

"Then where? Your room?"

"What happens if he wakes up and you're not here?" he asked.

"I tol' you, he won't wake up," she said. "When he gets like this, ya can't wake him."

"He dozed off in my room and woke up right away."

"He ain't dozin' this time," she said. "He's dead asleep." She grabbed his hand. "Come on."

"Where are we going?"

"Someplace where he couldn't hear us if he wanted to," she assured him.

He followed Jada to the livery stable. They went in through a back door and she hurriedly lit a lamp. Then she pulled off her clothes and stood before him naked. The golden light given off by the lamp made her look like she was glowing.

"I want you," she said. "I want you to take me."

"Jada—"

"That's the only way I'm gonna help ya," she said. "You're gonna leave this town soon, ain't ya?"

"Probably tomorrow."

"Then this is my last chance," she said. "Ain't gonna be nothin' like this for me after you leave here."

She turned, went into one of the stalls, bent over with her back to him, and started fluffing up some hay. He couldn't help but stare. She had an exquisitely shaped backside, powerful thighs and legs.

When she turned back to him she put her hands behind her back, thrusting out her breasts, and stared at him.

"Ya ain't gonna leave me here all hot, bothered, and naked, are you, Clint?" she asked. "That would be a terrible thing ta do to a girl."

"No," he said, resigned to his fate, "I'm not going to do that, Jada."

TWELVE

When Clint went back to his hotel room, he was exhausted from trying to keep up with Jada. The girl had an insatiable appetite for sex, and Clint wondered how she managed to go without for so long.

He'd had to peel her off of him in order to get to his room so he could go to sleep. He warned her that she had better keep her part of the bargain and have Antoine ready to talk by the next morning.

"Don't worry," she told him. "You gave me what I needed, so tomorrow I'll get you what you need."

When he woke the next morning, he quickly got dressed and walked over to Antoine and Jada's shack. He found it empty. The furniture was still there, but all the clothes were gone. He walked around the building, then went over to the livery. There was an old white man there, about sixty, who looked up as Clint entered.

"Do you know where Antoine is?" he asked.

"Gone," the old man said.

"What do you mean, gone?"

"Gone," the man said. "He left. Him and the girl."

"What about the livery stable?"

"He give it to me, along with the shack, only I ain't moved inta the shack yet. Gotta do that later today, with my clothes and things—"

"Wait a minute," Clint said. "He didn't sell it to you? He just gave it to you?"

"That's right."

"Why?"

The man shrugged. "I dunno. He said him and the girl had ta leave. Say, are you the fella with the big black horse?"

"That's right."

"Beautiful animal. Ya gonna leave him here long?"

"No," Clint said. "As a matter of fact, I'm taking him now."

"Oh." The man looked disappointed.

"Get him ready for me, will you?" Clint asked. "I'll be back right after I've had some breakfast and talked to the sheriff."

"Sure thing."

Clint turned and left, completely baffled. Why would Antoine and Jada have left town rather than talk to him?

"They did what?" Benny asked.

"They left town."

"Just like that?"

"Yes."

Benny put a couple of hard-boiled eggs on the bar for

Clint, who picked one up and started rolling it to loosen the shell.

"Why would they do that?" Benny asked.

"Organ Pipe."

"What about it?"

"Antoine was going to tell me something this morning, something about Organ Pipe."

"Who told you that?"

"Jada," Clint said. "He said earlier that he had something to tell me about the place, and when I brought him home last night, she said she'd sober him up this morning and find out what it was, only now they're gone."

"What about the livery?"

"Gave it away to some old man."

"That must be Louie," Benny said. "He's Antoine's best friend."

"Well, I guess he *was* Antoine's best friend." Clint finished peeling the shell from the egg and took a bite. At that moment Benny went in the back and returned with a cup of coffee for Clint. He finished the first egg, washed it down with some coffee, and started peeling the second.

"I don't understand this," Benny said.

"You know," Clint said, "I think you do. I think you do understand it. See, I think everybody in this town knows about Organ Pipe, and nobody wants to tell me about it."

"Why would they do that?"

"You tell me." Clint ate half the egg.

"Clint, I'm tellin' ya," Benny said, "I don't know anything about a place called Organ Pipe."

"Benny the Bull," Clint said, "you and everybody else in this town are liars—but that's okay." He ate the rest of the egg. "I'm leaving town, and I'll find out about Organ Pipe on my own. Thanks for the eggs."

"Clint—"

"No, it's okay," Clint said. He finished his coffee. "I'm going to the livery right now and riding out. Goodbye to Miller's Crossing and all twenty-two of you. Oh wait, now it's twenty!"

THIRTEEN

Clint rode into Yuma three days later. He had not pushed Eclipse at all, and had also stopped off in the town of Rosewood first for that cold beer. He'd ridden in, drank the beer, and ridden out again. He hadn't asked anyone there about a town called Organ Pipe. In fact, he had forgotten all about it.

Yuma was the largest town he'd been in for quite a while. He intended to take advantage of it. A good hotel, a bath, some new clothes, more cold beer, and some good meals.

And a good livery stable for Eclipse, so he could be pampered.

He found the hotel and stable on the same street.

"Give him the best," he told the livery owner.

"You bet," the man said. "That's what a horse like this deserves, mister."

Clint slapped the big Darley Arabian on the neck,

then took his saddlebags and rifle and headed for the Coronado Hotel.

Freshly bathed, with his rifle and saddlebags in his room, he went out in search of that first good meal. He decided against the hotel dining room for that. He'd try it later.

He found a small café that had wonderful smells coming out the front door. He went in, was shown to a table, and ordered a steak with all the trimmings. When he asked if they served beer, the waiter said yes, so he ordered one, "Very cold."

"Comin' up, sir," the waiter said.

The steak and beer were excellent, and so was the pie he followed them up with. His only complaint was the coffee, but that was often the case. He was very picky about his coffee.

He paid the check and went out onto the street. There were a couple of hours of daylight left, and he hadn't been to Yuma in a long time, so he decided to walk around town. He figured his last stop would be at the sheriff's office, a courtesy call just to let the man know he was in town.

Yuma was bustling, much too busy and fast-growing a town for him to want to live in. He still preferred places like Labyrinth, Texas, where he tended to spend his time when he wasn't on the trail. Even it was beginning to expand, but it was still small enough for him to be able to relax in.

There was not an empty storefront to be seen in Yuma, and every store seemed to be doing a brisk business.

There were enough people walking the streets that, every so often, Clint had to be careful not to bump into them. As empty and desolate as Miller's Crossing had been, Yuma was the opposite. Only the presence of hot meals and cold beer swung Clint's preference Yuma's way.

He stopped at the sheriff's office, which was a new two-story brick building. Clint might have thought it was a more modern police department but for the sign outside that actually said "SHERIFF'S OFFICE."

Inside he found a spacious, clean room with not one but two gun racks, both filled with weapons that looked recently cleaned and oiled. There were three men at two desks that were set up to face each other. Behind one of the desks was the staircase to the second floor. The men were all wearing the same uniform, brown shirts and trousers and shiny boots. They also wore cavalry holsters on their hips.

"Help ya, friend?" the oldest of the three men asked.

Clint approached him. Although he was older, the man seemed to be just another of the deputies, and not the sheriff.

"Sheriff around?" Clint asked.

"Not right now," the man said. "I'm Senior Deputy Fellows, this is Deputy Stone and Deputy Bennett."

"Glad to meet you all," Clint said. "My name is Clint Adams."

"*The* Clint Adams?" Deputy Stone asked.

"The Gunsmith?" Deputy Bennett asked.

"That's right," Clint said to both of them.

"Wow!" Stone said. He was the youngest of the deputies, probably in his mid-twenties.

"Fellas, why don't you go and make your rounds?" Fellows suggested.

"We just did our rounds, Fred," Bennett said.

"Well, do them again," Fellows said. "Mr. Adams and me are gonna have a talk."

"Why can't we stay?" Stone asked.

"Out!" Fellows said.

Grumbling, the two deputies grabbed their hats and went out the door.

"All right, Mr. Adams," Deputy Fellows asked, "what's on your mind?"

FOURTEEN

"Can I have a seat?" Clint asked.

"Sure," the head deputy said. "Pull up a chair."

Clint pulled a straight-backed wooden chair over and sat opposite the deputy, who had positioned himself behind the desk.

"I just rode into town earlier today, Deputy," Clint said. "Got a room, had a bath and a meal and a turn around town. Haven't been to Yuma in a long time. Looks like it's booming."

"It's growin' quick, that's for sure," Deputy Fellows said. "What brings you here, Mr. Adams?"

"Just passing through, Deputy," Clint said. "I've been on the trail for a while, got kind of tired and decided to stop here. I was in Miller's Crossing for a day—"

"Miller's Crossing?" Fellows asked. "Is that town still alive?"

"Twenty people," Clint said, "but still going."

"I never woulda guessed," Fellows said, shaking his head. "That fella Benny still the sheriff?"

"Sheriff, undertaker, saloon owner, bartender . . ." Clint said.

"Sounds like he's five of the twenty people."

"Well, there were twenty-two people living there when I got there, but two left."

"Guess the other twenty will, too, eventually."

"So where's the sheriff off to?"

"Actually," the deputy said, "he's out of town, tracking a couple of would-be bank robbers who killed a teller."

"He's tracking them alone?"

"No, he took another deputy with him," Fellows said. "I wanted to go with him, but he said I had to stay behind and be in charge."

"Guess that's what a senior deputy is supposed to do. Who is the sheriff, by the way?"

"His name is Bockwinkle," Fellows said, "Nick Bockwinkle. Been sheriff here about two years."

"And how long have you been here?"

"I've been a deputy about eighteen months—senior deputy for five."

"When did the sheriff leave?"

"Several days ago," Fellows said. "No idea how long he'll be away."

"Well, it doesn't matter," Clint said. "I was just stopping in to tell the sheriff I was in town."

"So you told me," Fellows said. "You wouldn't be here lookin' for trouble, would ya, Mr. Adams?"

"No, Deputy," Clint said. "Despite what you might think about me, I don't go looking for trouble."

"But it manages to find you, doesn't it?"

"That I can't argue with," Clint said, standing up. "But I do my best to avoid it."

"That's good to hear," Fellows said. "How long you think you'll be in Yuma?"

"I don't know," Clint said. "A couple of days, maybe. I guess we'll just have to see."

"Would you mind lettin' me know when you're ready to leave?" Fellows asked. "Just so I can stop listenin' for shots?"

"I'll let you know, Deputy," Clint promised. "I'll let you know."

Clint left the sheriff's office and stopped in at the first saloon he came to, the Dusty Trail. He ordered a cold beer after elbowing himself a spot at the crowded bar. It was getting on toward dusk, and every chair and table was full. One table sported four guards from nearby Yuma Prison, drinking, laughing, and playing grab-ass with one of the saloon girls.

The place was noisy, and for a moment Clint found himself longing for the silence of the saloon in Miller's Crossing. What he needed was a cross between the two. He finished his beer and went off in search of it.

Eventually, he came to a small saloon called the Wagon Wheel. It even had a big wheel above the front door. As Clint entered, he saw that it was only about half-full, and seemed to have only a bartender and one girl working the floor. Half the tables were empty, and there was plenty of room at the bar. If it had cold beer, this would be the place for him.

"Help ya?" the barman asked.

"Got cold beer?"

"Definitely," the man said. He drew one and set it in front of Clint. "That do ya?"

Clint sipped it, and enjoyed the feel of the cold liquid moving down his throat.

"This'll do," he said, looking around, "this'll do just fine."

FIFTEEN

As the two deputies left the sheriff's office, Deputy Stone said, "Wow. The Gunsmith in our town. Whataya think of that?"

"I think I wonder what he's doin' here," Deputy Bennett said. "The Gunsmith don't just come to a town for no reason."

"Maybe he's lookin' for somebody," Stone said.

"Yeah, but who?" Bennett asked.

"Whoever it is," Stone said. "I'm glad I ain't them. Look, are we really gonna make rounds again so soon?"

"Why don't we switch up?" Bennett suggested. "You make mine and I'll make yours this time."

"Okay," Stone said. "I don't mind that."

"I don't either," Bennett said. "I'll see ya later, Dan."

"Okay, Teddy."

Teddy Bennett watched Dan Stone go off to make his rounds, then turned and headed the other way. Switching their rounds would enable him to go and see a man who would find Clint Adams's presence in Yuma very interesting.

Mike Callum sat at a table alone in the back of the Red Bear Saloon. He drank there because it was one of Yuma's smaller drinking establishments, with no dancing, music, or gambling to distract from the business of drinking. He also liked the painting behind the bar of a red grizzly bear standing up on its hind legs. He often thought that the look on the bear's face reflected how he felt inside.

Callum was forty-two, and figured Yuma was his last stop on a life that had seen him chasing a reputation at every turn. The only reputation he'd managed to cultivate was as a man nobody in Yuma wanted to drink with. Well, that was fine with him. He didn't want to drink with any of them, either. But Callum knew something about himself that nobody else knew. He was good with a gun, maybe the best he'd ever seen, but he'd never had a chance to prove it—not in public, where everyone could see. He'd done everything from being a cowboy to being a lawman, with stops at bounty hunter, range detective, and outlaw in between. He'd outdrawn and killed men with reputations, but he only had his own word for that.

He poured himself another whiskey. He was about two more glasses from being cross-eyed drunk, but he was in no hurry. He liked the slow ascent to that kind of oblivion, and he liked to be able to taste the whiskey all the way. The only time he didn't like the taste of whiskey was when it was stale on his tongue in the morning.

That was why he kept an open bottle by his bed, so he could refresh the taste as soon as he woke up.

Mike Callum also figured he was about the width of a cunt hair from being the town drunk.

When Deputy Teddy Bennett entered the Red Bear, he immediately spotted Mike Callum sitting in the back, working on a bottle of whiskey. He had no idea how many bottles had been drunk that day, but he hoped his friend was still conscious. He'd seen the man drink with his eyes open before, while unconscious.

He walked to the back and sat down opposite Callum. The man looked across at him blearily, but was still somewhat conscious.

"Hey, Mike," Bennett said.

"Teddy?" Callum said. "Hey, Teddy Bennett, my only friend in Yuma. Hell, my only friend anywhere." Callum found that funny and began to cackle.

"Mike, come on," Bennett said. "I got somethin' important to tell ya, and ya gotta be able to hear me."

"Hear ya?" Callum asked. "Hell, I can hear ya, Teddy. Ya wanna drink?"

"No, I don't want a drink," Bennett said. "I'm on duty."

"Hey, that's right," Callum said. "My friend Teddy is a deputy!"

"A deputy with news for you, Mike," Bennett said. "News you been waitin' for your whole life."

"My whole life?" Callum asked, squinting at Bennett across the table.

"Yeah, Mike, your whole life. Listen, I'm gonna get you some coffee and then we're gonna talk."

"Talk?"

"Right."

"Coffee?"

"Right again."

"I don't want no coffee."

"Well, you're gonna have some," Bennett said, standing up. "Just don't move till I get back."

Callum squinted at his friend again, and then as Bennett walked over to the bar to get some coffee, he shouted, "And get me another bottle, too."

SIXTEEN

After half a dozen cups of coffee, Mike Callum put his hands out in front of his face and said, "Enough! Enough! I'm drowning in coffee."

"You ain't never drowned in whiskey, Mike, so I doubt yer gonna drown in coffee," Teddy Bennett said, but he put the pot down without pouring yet another cup.

"Ooh," Callum said, holding his head, "now I got a headache I ain't even enjoyed gettin'."

"Never mind your headache," Bennett said. "You'll forget about it when I tell ya what I got ta tell ya."

"And what is that?" Callum asked. "What's so all-fired important that you had to interrupt a perfectly good drunk?"

"Clint Adams?"

Callum released his head and looked across the table at Bennett.

"What?"

"Clint Adams?" Bennett said. "The Gunsmith?"

"What about him?"

"He's here."

Callum looked around.

"I mean here in town," Bennett said, "not here in this saloon."

"What's he doin' in town?" Callum asked.

"I don't know," Bennett said. "He stopped by to see the sheriff, and the senior deputy ran us off before we could hear what he wanted."

"What'd the sheriff say?"

"He ain't around," Bennett said. "Him and another deputy took off after them bank robbers."

"Any idea how long he's stayin'?" Callum asked.

"I tol' ya," Bennett said, "I didn't hear nothin' that he had to say."

"Well, I ain't in any shape to face him tonight, or in the mornin'," Callum said. He reached across and grabbed Bennett's sleeve. "Find out what's goin' on for me, Teddy. How long he's stayin' in town, what he wants. As much as you kin get, hear?"

"I hear ya, Mike," Bennett said, "but when I leave here, don't go divin' back inta the bottle."

"Don't worry," Callum said. "I only drink when I got no reason not to—and you just give me a reason."

After Deputy Bennett left, Callum went to the bar and got himself a cold beer. For a man who drank as heavily as he did, beer was hardly drinking.

He took the beer back to his table and nursed it while thinking over what Bennett had told him.

Whatever reason Clint Adams was in Yuma, this was

Mike Callum's chance to finally prove himself, finally get himself a reputation and change his life. All he had to do was be fast enough.

He looked down at his hands, which, at that moment, were trembling. He grabbed the beer and drank down half of it, then set the mug down and looked at his hands again. Better, but not perfect.

Suddenly, he became aware of the sour smell of his own sweat; he touched his face and felt the stubble there. He had to go to bed. In the morning he'd have a good breakfast, then a bath and a shave, then maybe a little hair of the dog just to settle his nerves a bit.

After that he'd find out from Bennett why Clint Adams was in town, and how long he was intending to stay. It would be better for Callum if he had a few days to work with, but if all he had was tomorrow, he'd have to make the best of it.

But first he'd finish his beer. After all, he'd paid for it.

Later that night Clint Adams entered his hotel room, looking forward to a good night's sleep. He'd had a few beers in the Wagon Wheel, where he'd been able to drink them in peace, at his own leisure. If he spent another night in Yuma, maybe he'd look for a poker game, or drink somewhere more lively, like the Dusty Trail, but at the moment he wanted to go to bed.

He reached for the dirty shirt he'd been wearing when he arrived. It was lying on top of the bed. He'd have to get it washed. As he picked it up, he felt something crumpled in the pocket. When he took it out, he saw that it was the note he'd collected from the wind before getting to Miller's Crossing. He'd forgotten about the note, and about Organ Pipe.

He smoothed it out and read it again. Then he read the stories on both sides. Nothing exciting there. The only thing of interest on either side was the childish scrawl that said, "Please help us."

He smoothed out the paper some more and put it on the table next to the bed. Surely, in a town the size of Yuma, someone would have heard of a town called Organ Pipe.

He'd ask some questions in the morning.

SEVENTEEN

Clint had breakfast in the hotel dining room the next morning. While he was eating his bacon and eggs, an idea occurred to him. When he'd finished his breakfast, he paid his check, left the hotel, and walked to the office of the *Yuma Daily Sun*.

As he entered the newspaper office, he could hear the press operating. It was a deafening sound, and the man operating the press hadn't heard him come in. Clint looked around, and saw some more men behind a glass partition in an office. They were in a heated conversation. He looked for the door to the office, found it, and opened it.

". . . once I've told you a thousand times, check your sources, Lou," one man was saying. "If I had run that story without checking, it would have embarrassed me and the newspaper. I can't have that kind of carelessness."

"Gimme another chance, Mr. Wynn," the other man said. "One more."

"I've given you enough chances, Lou," Wynn said. "I'm done. We're done."

"Ya can't fire me!"

"I just did, Lou."

The man Clint assumed was the newspaper's editor—after all, he was firing someone—was tall and white-haired, with remarkably unlined skin. When Clint got a better look, he realized that the man's hair wasn't white because he was old. He was closer to forty than sixty.

The other fellow was in his fifties, a small, slovenly man who was sweating heavily.

"You're too experienced to be making these mistakes, Lou," Wynn said. "I've got to assume that you're losing it."

"Mr. Wynn, please—"

"We're done here, Lou." The editor turned to Clint. "Can I help you, friend?"

The fired man stood there for a moment, then turned and skulked out the door.

"I assume you're the editor?" Clint said.

"That's right. My name's Steve Wynn. You're not a reporter looking for a job, are you?"

"Sorry, no."

"Too bad. Who are you?"

"My name's Clint Adams."

"Clint Adams?" Wynn said. "The Gunsmith? Jesus Christ, how the hell did you get into town without me knowi—Wait a minute. Are you really Clint Adams?"

"Doesn't really matter if you believe me or not, Mr.

Wynn," Clint said. "I'm not going to try to prove it to you. I just have a question."

"Wait, wait," Wynn said, excitedly. "You are the Gunsmith, right?"

"Yes, I am."

"Well, this is great!" Wynn said. "You just come walking into my paper? This is great."

"Mr. Wynn—"

"We can do an interview right now," Wynn said, apparently looking around for a pad of paper. "Course, I just fired my only reporter, but it hasn't been so long since I—"

"A newspaper in a town this size and you only had one reporter?" Clint asked.

"I had two," Wynn said. "One was killed last week, and I just fired the other one. Ah, here." He grabbed some paper and a pencil and turned to Clint.

"Mr. Wynn, I'm not here for an interview."

"That's okay," Wynn said. "You want some time to form your thoughts?"

"No," Clint said, "I mean I didn't come in here to give you an interview. I came in to ask you a question."

"Well, okay," Wynn said, "but can we do an interview later?"

"I'd rather not."

"But it would be good for you," Wynn said. "You could let people know who the real Clint Adams is."

"Why do you think anyone would believe what you write in your paper about me?"

"Because it'll come straight from your mouth."

"And what makes you think they'll believe me?"

"Well ... whether they believe you or not, I'll sell some papers."

"So then you don't care if I tell you the truth or not in this interview."

"Then you'll do it?"

"You're missing my point," Clint said. "No, I won't do an interview."

Wynn stared at him and his face fell.

"Sure," he said, "why should today be different? No reporter, nothing to write." The man sat heavily in his desk chair, looking up at Clint. "All right, so what's your question?"

"Have you ever heard of a town called Organ Pipe?" Clint asked. "Or a newspaper called the *Organ Pipe Register*?"

EIGHTEEN

Mike Callum woke with a pounding head, a scratchy throat, and a thick tongue. He reached for the bottle by the bed, checked himself before taking a huge swallow, and instead just took a little nip. He then put the top back on the bottle and left it on the night table.

He staggered to his dresser, poured water from a pitcher into a basin, and washed. That was just to get started. He dressed and went down to get some breakfast, which he'd follow with a bath, a shave, and a haircut.

If Clint Adams managed to kill him, he was going to be a presentable corpse.

Editor Steve Wynn walked to the office door, opened it, and shouted until the pressman heard him.

"Take a break," he said.

"How long?"

"Half an hour."

"But I gotta—"

"Just go!"

He slammed the door and returned to Clint, who had taken a seat.

"Organ Pipe," he said.

"That's right."

"The *Register*, you said?"

"Yes."

"Do you have—"

Clint held the newspaper scrap out to him. Wynn studied it, both sides, read the scrawled message.

"Let's talk about an interview," he said.

"Let's not."

"Fine," Wynn said. He handed the scrap back to Clint. "I don't know anything."

"You're lying."

"Oh?"

"A lot of people are lying to me," Clint said. "What's so special about this place that people lie about knowing where or what it is?"

The editor sat back in his chair, which creaked.

"You think people are lying to you?" he asked. "Everybody?"

"Well . . . a lot of people," Clint said. "Everybody I talk to can't be so ignorant of this place."

"You are."

"Yes, but—"

"And correct me if I'm wrong, but you've traveled extensively throughout the West."

"Yes, I have."

"Then why haven't you heard of it?"

"Look," Clint said, "you're a newspaperman. You must have heard of this newspaper."

"Must I have?" asked Wynn.

"Yeah," Clint said, "you must have."

"Well then, if I know something," Wynn said, "let's discuss a trade for it."

"You want an interview."

"Obviously."

"Why?"

"Because you're news," Wynn said.

"I'm old news."

"Not so old," Wynn said. "Everybody knows who the Gunsmith is. Everybody wants to know what you think, what you're doing, why you've done the things you've done."

Clint thought a moment, then said, "I'll tell you what I'll do."

"What?"

"You tell me what I want to know," Clint said.

"And what do I get?"

"You get to ask me questions."

Wynn sat back in his chair.

"That sounds oddly like an interview," Steve Wynn said.

"On one condition."

"What's that?"

"I'm always being asked for an interview," Clint said. "And people always have the same questions."

"I'll bet they do."

"So I'll only answer your questions," Clint said, "if you can come up with one—just one—that I've never heard before."

Wynn considered the terms.

"Okay," he said, "done."

"Okay," Clint said, "what do you know about a place called Organ Pipe?"

"Nothing."

"Then this isn't going to work."

"But I know somebody who might know."

"Who?"

"A man named Hickey," Wynn said, "Joe Hickey."

"And where do I find Joe Hickey?"

"Close by," Wynn said, "very close by."

NINETEEN

Clint and Steve Wynn were admitted to the office of Paul Kelsey, the warden of Yuma Territorial Prison. A large, florid-faced man in his sixties, Kelsey stood and extended his hand from behind his desk.

"Steve, it's good to see you," Kelsey said. "What brings you out here?"

"Warden," Wynn said, "this is Clint Adams."

The warden stopped a moment, then moved his hand over to Clint, who shook it.

"Well, I heard you were bringing someone with you, but I had no idea it would be the Gunsmith. A pleasure, sir. Have a seat, please."

Both men took seats and the warden sat down behind his desk.

"Now, what can I do for you gentlemen?" he asked.

"Joe Hickey," Wynn said.

"What about him?"

"Clint, here, would like to talk to him."

"Oh? What about?"

"It's personal," Clint said. So many people had acted odd when he mentioned Organ Pipe that he'd decided to keep the details to himself.

"I see. Do you know Hickey?"

"No."

"I see. I don't have any objection to you seeing him," the warden said, "but Hickey might. I'll have to go and ask him."

"While you're at it, Warden," Wynn said, "why don't you ask him if he'd do it as a favor to me?"

"Well, your paper did speak on his behalf during his trial," the warden said. "He might do it for that reason. I'll still have to go and ask him."

"We can wait," Clint said.

"Yes, well," Kelsey said, standing, "I'll just go and see, then. Can I get you gents something while you wait? Coffee? Whiskey?"

"We're fine," Clint said.

"I'll be a few minutes, then," the warden said.

As Kelsey left the office, Wynn said, "I could've used a whiskey."

"I get what I want from Hickey, I'll buy you as many as you want."

"One's my limit," Wynn said. "I have a little trouble if I go beyond that. Tend to lose jobs. You know, get myself fired."

"But this is your paper, isn't it?"

"No," he said. "I'm the editor. It's owned by . . . somebody else. I could still get my ass fired."

"Well," Clint said, "I wouldn't want to contribute to that."

"I appreciate that."

"So, tell me about you and Hickey."

"Nothing to tell," Wynn said. "I was one of the few who didn't think he was guilty."

"So another innocent man goes to prison?"

"Oh, he's not innocent," Wynn said. "I just don't think he was guilty of the murder he's in here serving time for. He is a killer, though. Even he admits that."

"And what about the warden?"

"I did a nice write-up about him a while back," Wynn said. "You know, about the improvements he'd made here at Yuma since he took over."

"How long has he been warden?" Clint asked.

"A year," Wynn said.

"And is he doing a good job?"

"As good as anyone can do," Wynn said. "The men are eating better than they used to, and have better visitation rights."

"I see."

"He's also pushing for something he calls 'conjugal visits.'"

"Conjugal . . . what?"

"He thinks that prisoners should be allowed to spend time with their wives once a month."

"Spend time with? You mean . . ."

"That's what I mean," the editor said. "Sex."

"That's kind of radical thinking for a warden, isn't it?"

"It is," Wynn said, "but it would probably make him the most popular warden in the history of the penal system—in any country."

"I can see why it would," Clint said.

The door opened at that moment and Warden Kelsey reentered the room.

"He'll see you, Mr. Adams. Come this way."

Wynn stood up with Clint and moved toward the door, but Kelsey blocked his way.

"Just Mr. Adams," he said.

"Why?" Wynn asked.

"I don't know, Steve," Kelsey said. "I'm just tellin' you what he said."

Wynn looked at Clint and said, "Okay, then, good luck. I'll see you when you get out."

"This way," the warden said.

TWENTY

As they walked down the hall, the warden asked Clint, "Do you know anything about Joe Hickey?"

"Just that he might be in here for a murder he didn't commit," Clint said.

"That's probably true," Warden Kelsey said, "but he's probably in here for all the murders he did commit and never got caught for."

"Does that sit right with you?" Clint asked.

"Why wouldn't it?"

"Mr. Wynn indicated to me that you might be a little . . . radical in your thinking. Not really like any other wardens I might have known."

"That's true enough," Kelsey said. "I don't think these men have to be treated like animals just because they're behind bars."

"I'm sure they appreciate your thinking."

"There aren't many of them who take me seriously," Kelsey said, then added, "yet."

"Hickey one of the ones that does?"

"Hickey and I get along," Kelsey said, "and he has a lot of influence on the prison population. When he talks, they tend to listen. Or they stop listenin'—sometimes permanently."

"Sounds like you and him might have a special relationship."

"We might," the warden said, "one day."

They went down several hallways and—Clint swore—a tunnel or two before reaching a wooden door with a small barred window. There was a guard standing in front of it.

"Open it," the warden said.

"Yes, sir."

The guard produced a key and unlocked the door. As he opened it and Clint started in, the warden put his hand on Clint's arm to stop him.

"I'll need your gun," the man said.

Clint hesitated, but he understood and handed the weapon over.

"You have any trouble in there, just yell out and the guard will come in."

"Okay."

Clint walked through the door.

The prisoner was seated at a wooden table, his wrists shackled together, his ankles shackled together, and then his wrists and ankles connected by a chain. He was once a big man, but had lost a lot of weight recently. His prison stripes hung on him. He had a prison pallor, but seemed relatively healthy. Clint thought that a few meals would do wonders for him, bring him back to health. He seemed to be in his late forties, but might have been younger. His face was black with stubble.

"You him?" he asked. "You the Gunsmith?"

"That's me," Clint said. "Clint Adams. You're Joe Hickey?"

"That's right. Siddown, why don't ya?" Hickey said. "Make yerself comfortable."

There was one other chair, at the opposite end of the five-foot table. Clint sat.

"Took your gun, huh?"

"Yup."

"As you can see," Hickey said, moving his hands and rattling his chains, "I can't do nothin' anyway."

"Guess they just wanted to be sure."

"I don't get too many visitors," Hickey said, "and none as famous as you. What brings ya here?"

"Organ Pipe." Clint decided to get right to the point.

"What?"

"Have you ever heard of a place called Organ Pipe?" Clint asked.

Hickey sat back in his chair and stared at Clint.

"What are ya askin' me about that fer?"

Clint shrugged. "I'm curious."

"That kinda curious could get ya killed."

"So you have heard of it?"

"Sure."

"You're the first person I've talked to who's admitted that the place exists."

"Existed."

"What?"

"It don't exist," Hickey said. "It existed."

"What—what happened to it?"

"Organ Pipe was wiped out years ago."

"Wiped out?" Clint repeated. "Wiped out by what?"

"Mister," Hickey said, "believe me, you don't wanna go there."

"Why not?"

"Organ Pipe was wiped out," Hickey said, "by a plague."

TWENTY-ONE

"What the hell are you talking about?" Clint asked.

"Organ Pipe, Arizona, right?" Hickey asked.

"All I know is Organ Pipe," Clint said. "Could there be two towns with that name?"

"Well, I suppose there could be," Hickey said. "Maybe after the first town died, they started one up somewhere else with the same name."

"Are you sure about this?"

"That newspaper editor brought you here, right?" Hickey asked.

"That's right."

"Well, that's because nobody knows this area like I do," Hickey said.

"Can you tell me where Organ Pipe was?" Clint asked.

"You actually wanna go there?" Hickey asked. "Why?"

Clint took the newspaper clipping out and passed it to the shackled man.

"Somebody wrote a note on here?" Hickey asked.

"That's what it looks like."

"How did you get it?"

"It blew into my camp one morning."

"This note? But this is an old newspaper."

"I know."

"You think this has been blowin' around Arizona all this time?"

"I don't know what to think, Hickey," Clint said. "But somebody needed enough help to write that and toss it into the wind."

"Well," Hickey said, putting the clipping down on the table carefully, "that town needed help, all right. If I was you, I wouldn't be carryin' that around too long. Might have plague attached to it."

"What kind of plague are we talking about, Hickey?" Clint asked.

"The kind that can kill a whole town, that's what kind," Hickey said. "Ain't no use in going to that town, Adams. It's dead."

"Just tell me where it is," Clint said, "and I'll go and see for myself."

"Well, it's kinda hard to tell you where it is," Hickey said, "but I can show you."

"Which means you want me to get you out of here," Clint observed.

"That would be helpful."

"That's not going to happen, Hickey," Clint said.

"The state is not going to let you out of prison just to satisfy a curiosity of mine." Clint stood up. "So I guess we're done here."

Hickey rattled his chains and said, "Wait, wait, don't be in such a damned hurry!"

Clint stopped, and saw the guard peering in through the bars to see what the commotion was. He waved the man away and turned back to Hickey.

"Sit back down," Hickey said. When Clint didn't move, the prisoner added, "Please."

Clint sat.

"The thing about Organ Pipe is where it's located. You could approach it for miles and not see it, and then there it was, right in front of you."

"It's hidden?"

"It's well hidden by the hills around it," Hickey said. "More people would find it by accident than would actually go there on purpose."

"But you could tell me how to find it?" Clint asked.

"I could tell you how to find where it used to be," Hickey said. "I'm sure they musta burned the whole thing to the ground."

Clint looked down at the newspaper article, which he'd forgotten to pick up again—or had he? Was Hickey telling the truth about a plague wiping out the town? Clint shook his head and picked up the clipping. He folded it under the watchful eye of the convict and put it back in his shirt pocket.

"Tell me how to find it," he said.

"Get me some paper and a pencil," Hickey said, "and

I'll draw you a map—but you gotta agree to somethin' first. I mean, I gotta get somethin' outta this, right?"

"What do you want?"

When Clint was finished with Hickey, a guard walked him back to the warden's office, where Steve Wynn and Warden Kelsey were sharing a whiskey and talking.

"Did you get what you wanted?" Wynn asked.

"I did."

"What did it cost you?" Kelsey asked.

"I'll be sending some packages in for Hickey from time to time, Warden," Clint said. "Will you see that he gets them?"

"As long as there are no weapons in them," Kelsey said, "I don't see why not."

TWENTY-TWO

When Clint and Wynn got back to town, Clint said, "Buy you that whiskey?"

"I had one with the warden," the editor said. "That's my limit, but I'll take a beer."

Clint let Wynn pick the place, and he chose the Wagon Wheel.

"It's quieter," the editor explained, "and closer to the paper."

They went inside, and found it fairly empty since it wasn't yet noon. The bartender greeted Wynn by name— "Mornin', Mr. Wynn"—and Clint and Steve ordered two beers.

"So," Wynn said, "what can you tell me that you didn't want to say in front of the warden?"

"Hickey wanted me to get him out so he could show me where Organ Pipe is."

"He knows?"

"He says he knows where it was."

"Was?"

"According to him," Clint said, "the town died of the plague. He thinks it was probably burned to the ground."

"That's odd."

"Why?"

"You'd think that would be newsworthy," Wynn said. "I never heard a word about it. So he told you where the town was?"

"Drew me a map."

"And you promised to send him some . . . items?"

"From time to time," Clint said.

"Like what?"

"Things he likes to eat," Clint said, "cigars, to-bacco . . . easy stuff, but things he can't get inside."

"Things he could use as currency inside, too."

"Whatever he wants to use them for, I don't care," Clint said.

"Where is this Organ Pipe supposed to have been?"

"Two days' ride south from here."

"You goin' alone?"

"Can't think of anybody I'd want to take with me," Clint said.

"How about a reporter?"

"You don't have a reporter," Clint reminded him. "You want to come yourself?"

"I can't leave the paper," Wynn said. "Shit!"

"That's okay," Clint said, "I don't really see the benefit to me to take a writer along. He'd just slow me down. But thanks for getting me in to see Hickey."

"Hey, don't forget, you owe me before you owe

Hickey," Wynn reminded him. "When were you planning on leaving?"

"In the morning."

"Then we better go over to the office and do this interview," Wynn said.

"Can't we do it when I get back?"

"And if you don't get back?" Wynn asked. "What do I do then?"

"Good point." Clint finished his beer, put the empty mug down on the bar. "I'm hungry. How about we do this thing over a steak lunch?"

"Sure. Why not?"

"You know a place makes a good steak?"

Wynn grinned and nodded, and put his half-finished beer down on the bar.

"I know just the place," he said. "Let's stop by the office so I can pick up a pencil and some paper, and then I'll take you over."

Over a delicious steak at a café the editor said had the best food in town, Clint tried his best to answer Steve Wynn's questions, but before they started, Wynn had to ask that one question Clint had never heard before.

"You know," Wynn said, when they sat down, "I gave this a lot of thought, came up with a few questions, but discarded them all. I'm sure they've been asked before."

Clint remained silent. He didn't want to give the man any hints.

"But I think I finally came up with one you haven't heard before."

"Okay, let's hear it."

Wynn sat back, looked across the table, and asked, "What's your favorite color?"

Clint stared at the man, then laughed and shook his head.

"You know, in all the years people have been asking me questions, you're right, nobody has ever asked me that," he admitted. "So go ahead, conduct your interview."

"Okay," Steve Wynn said, "then let's start with that one. What *is* your favorite color?"

"Red."

TWENTY-THREE

Steve Wynn fired questions at him for an hour, and he answered as truthfully as he could. There were times when a totally truthful answer might have incriminated him or someone else, so he had to be inventive. For the most part, though, he told the truth. And to his credit the editor came up with some other questions that had never been asked before.

Over pie and coffee Clint told Wynn, "That wasn't as bad as most."

"I guess I'll take that as a compliment," Wynn said.

"That's how I meant it. Sure you don't want to jump on a horse tomorrow and go looking for a town that died of the plague?"

"Oddly enough," Wynn said, "it's the jumping on a horse part of that that doesn't agree with me."

"Not afraid of the plague?"

"I still think if that was the case, a town dying like that, maybe being burned to the ground, it would've been big news. Burn a town to the ground—any size town—and that would have to make for a lot of smoke. Somebody would've had to see it."

"Well, I guess I'll find out when I get out there. With a word like 'plague' connected to it, maybe that's why folks have been unwilling to talk to me about Organ Pipe."

"What if Hickey has sent you on a wild-goose chase?" Wynn asked.

"That's something I'll deal with if the time comes," Clint said.

"And your reason for all this is still . . . what? Just curiosity?"

"Pretty much."

"And a cry for help."

Clint shrugged, pushed his empty pie dish away, and drank the last of his coffee.

"I think I'll go and talk to that senior deputy, see what he thinks of all this."

"That'd be Fellows, right? You think he was one of the ones who was lying to you?"

"Maybe," Clint said. "Let's see what he says now that I know what I know."

"Well, if you do find that the town was burned to the ground and died of the plague, you will give me the story, right?"

"Absolutely," Clint said. "After you run my interview, I'll want you to have a big story to make people forget it."

"I don't think that'll happen," Wynn said. "In fact, I kind of think some Eastern papers will want to pick it up."

"Great," Clint said.

"Tell you what," Wynn said. "I'll buy lunch to ease the blow."

"You've got a deal."

When Clint entered the two-story brick sheriff's office, the senior deputy, Fellows, was seated behind the desk, this time alone.

"Mr. Adams." He greeted Clint as he entered. "How have you been liking our fair town?"

"I like it fine."

"And your visit to the prison?"

"You heard about that, huh?"

"I try to keep my ears open."

"Then you must have heard who I went there to see."

"Well, since you took Mr. Wynn with you, and his paper was very vocal about Joe Hickey's conviction, I'm gonna guess it was Hickey. After all, Joe knows all of Arizona better than anybody I know."

"I'm glad to hear that," Clint said, "because he's drawn me a map to Organ Pipe."

"Organ Pipe?" Fellows said, frowning. "What's that?"

"It's a town . . . or it was, according to Hickey."

"A town? Around here?"

"Well, in Arizona, about two days from here."

Still frowning, Fellows said, "I don't think I've heard of the place."

"Well, it's supposed to have burned to the ground over two years ago."

"That would explain it, then," Fellows said. "Like I told you, I've only been here eighteen months."

"I'll bet your sheriff probably knows about it."

"I'll bet he does, but unfortunately we don't know when he'll be back."

"By the time he gets back, I might have all the answers I need," Clint said.

As Clint turned to leave, Fellows asked, "You leavin' town?"

"Tomorrow," Clint said, "but just to see if I can find Organ Pipe. I should be back within a week, either way."

"Stop in and let me know what happens, when you get back," Fellows said. "I'll be interested."

"Sure, Deputy," Clint said. "I'll see you soon."

TWENTY-FOUR

"Where'd you hear that Adams went to the prison?" Mike Callum asked Deputy Bennett.

"Deputy Fellows heard it," Bennett said, "an' he told me and Stone."

"What was he doin' at the prison?" Callum asked.

"I dunno," Bennett said. "Neither did Fellows. All we know is he went out there with the newspaper editor, um, Wynn?"

"Steve Wynn," Callum said. He scratched his head. "Only reason Wynn ever goes out there is to talk to Joe Hickey."

"What's the Gunsmith got to do with Joe Hickey?" Bennett asked.

"I don't know," Callum said, "but it's somethin' I got to find out before I kill 'im."

"You know Hickey, don't ya?"

"I know Joe Hickey real well," Mike Callum said. "Real well."

* * *

"You're pretty popular today, ain't ya?" the guard asked Joe Hickey as he led him from his cell.

"Who is it this time?" Hickey asked.

"That friend of yours, Mike Callum."

Callum was no friend of his, but he visited Hickey to stay on the right side of him, just in case he ever got out. If things went the state's way, though, not only would Hickey never get out, but his neck would get stretched. The only thing holding up his hanging so far was his lawyer, who was trying to make a name for himself.

"We're pretty much used ta you gettin' visited by that newspaper editor and this jasper, Callum. What did the Gunsmith want with you?"

"That's my business, ain't it?" Hickey said.

"Sure, Joe, sure," the guard said. "It's your business."

The guard took him to the same room, chained him up, and left him there. While he was waiting for the door to open, Hickey wondered what the hell Mike Callum wanted with him now.

When the door opened, Callum came right in and sat down across from Hickey.

"Joe," he said, "what the hell was the Gunsmith doin' here?"

"What's it to you?"

"I'm gonna kill 'im."

"You're gonna what?"

"You heard me," Callum said. "I'm gonna kill 'im."

"No, you ain't."

"What are you sayin'?" Callum asked. "You don't think I can?"

"Well, first, uh, no," Hickey said. "He'd kill you just as soon as look at ya. But second, even if you could kill 'im, I don't want you to."

"Why not?"

"Because I got a deal workin' with him, and I don't want you foulin' it up."

"What kind of deal?"

"The kind that just might get me out of here."

"You're in here for murder, Joe," Callum said. "What the hell could he do to get you out?"

"Well, for one," Hickey said, "he could do what none of my other so-called friends could do. He could break me out."

"Why would the Gunsmith break you out of prison?"

"Because I just may have somethin' he needs."

"Like what?"

"Well, now," Hickey said. "That's my business, ain't it?"

Callum leaned forward. "Look, Joe, I got a chance to make a name for myself," he said.

"You can make a name for yerself later, Mike," Hickey said. "I'm tellin' you not to mess up what I got goin' on. You hear?"

"Yeah, I heard," Callum said, "but fuck you, Joe."

"What did you say?"

"You heard me," Callum said. "You're in here and I'm out there. What are you gonna do to me?"

"Don't try me, Mike," Hickey said. "I'll reach out from in here—"

"How?" Callum asked. "You just said yourself your so-called friends are no good to you. So how you gonna reach out for me?"

Callum stood up and headed for the door. Behind him he heard Hickey's chains rattle as the man tried to stand up.

"Mike, so help me—"

"I was just showin' you some respect by comin' here, Joe," Callum said, "but to hell with you. You don't show me no respect at all, so fuck you."

"What the hell is wrong with you, Callum?" Hickey shouted. "Are you sober?"

Callum banged on the door for the guard. Hickey sat down in his chair as the guard let Callum out.

What was he worried about? There was no way Mike Callum could gun down the Gunsmith. No way.

Unless he did it from behind.

TWENTY-FIVE

Clint went to the livery to check on Eclipse and to tell the liveryman to have the horse ready first thing in the morning.

"Mister," the man said, "my first thing in the morning is nine because I drink a lot. What's yours?"

"You know, I'll have breakfast first and meet you here at nine," Clint said. "That's fine."

"I'll have him ready, mister," the man said, "but you're gonna bring him back, right? I mean, I ain't never had a horse like that in my house before."

"Your house?"

"This is my house," the man said. "Okay? I sleep in a damn shack, but this is my house."

"Okay, fine," Clint said. "Yeah, we'll be back in about a week."

"Okay," the man said. "You take good care of him now, all right?"

Clint didn't know how Eclipse turned men into nursemaids.

"I always take care of him," Clint said. "Don't worry."

As Clint left, the liveryman went back to Eclipse's stall to rub the big horse's neck and brush him—again.

Clint thought about leaving immediately, since there were hours of daylight left, but decided to leave it till morning. There was no emergency that he could see. Surely, whoever had written that note didn't still need help. If Joe Hickey was telling the truth, nobody from Organ Pipe needed help anymore.

Clint went to the Wagon Wheel and ordered a cold beer. He wondered if there were any survivors from Organ Pipe. He wondered what kind of disease had wiped the town out, and how long after the town burned down the site would hold the infection.

If Joe Hickey was telling the truth, Clint needed to talk to a doctor.

Dr. Frank Wheeler listened to Clint's question and then asked, "Are you talking about bubonic plague? Anthrax?"

"Actually, Doctor," Clint said, "I don't know what I'm talking about."

The white-haired older man studied him for a moment.

"Well," the doctor said, "if the site has been burned and some years have gone by, I don't think you'd be in any danger. But . . . why would you want to go there?"

"Let's just say once my curiosity is raised, I have to do something to satisfy it." Plus, somebody had written a note asking for help. "Doc, have you ever heard of a town called Organ Pipe?"

"Organ Pipe?" the doctor repeated. "No, I don't think so."

"You know," Clint said, "you're one of the only people I've asked who's told me no who I believe."

"Why would I lie about something like that?" the old sawbones asked.

"I don't know why anyone would lie," Clint said. "But I'm going to find out what's true, and what isn't. Thanks, Doc."

"Sure."

"Do I owe you anything?"

"For asking a question?" the doc asked. "Nothing."

Clint left the doctor's office feeling slightly better about finding the town of Organ Pipe. At least he wasn't riding into an infected site.

Still, why take the risk? All he had to do was get close enough to see if there was any rubble left, then turn around and ride away. If there was no town left, there was nobody needing help, and the note was just something that had been blowing in the wind for a couple of years.

Why was it that the older he got, the harder it seemed to get to turn his back on a cry for help, whether it came from a friend, a stranger, or a message on the wind?

Who appointed him savior of the world?

*   *   *

He had three beers at the Wagon Wheel and then went back to his hotel. In his room he read the note again, which was easy since it was only three words.

Tear it up, he thought, throw it away and forget the whole thing.

Instead he put it back in his saddlebag, pulled off his boots, and reclined on the bed. He put his hands behind his neck and stared at the ceiling. When he woke the next morning, the ceiling looked exactly the same.

TWENTY-SIX

Clint was having breakfast when Deputy Fellows walked into the hotel dining room. He saw Clint and walked over to his table.

"Coffee?" Clint asked.

"Why not?"

Fellows pulled up a chair. There was another cup on the table, so Clint picked up the pot and poured.

"Thanks."

"Breakfast?"

"Already had it," Fellows said. "At eight."

"What brings you here?"

"I don't know, exactly," Fellows said. "I guess I still don't have it straight in my mind why you want to look for this town that may have been burned to the ground because of some disease."

"Well," Clint said, "when you say it out loud like that, it just sounds like a stupid idea."

"That's what I thought."

"And I've been trying to figure that out for myself," Clint said. "Then I thought, maybe I'll never find it. Maybe I'm just giving it too much thought right now. I mean, if I don't find the town, there's no decision to make, is there?"

"I guess not."

"So I'll go looking for it, and if I find it, then I'll decide what I want to do about it."

"Probably a wiser decision," Fellows said. "I have a suggestion though."

"What's that?"

"We have a doctor in town named Wheeler," Fellows said. "Have a talk with him about diseases."

"I already did," Clint said, "but thanks."

Fellows gulped down his coffee and stood up.

"Then I guess I'm done here," he said. "Good luck, Mr. Adams. If you do come back here, let me know what happened, will you?"

"I will," Clint said, "if you'll call me Clint."

"Sure," Fellows said, "and my name is Fred."

"Maybe your sheriff will be here when I get back," Clint said.

"He's a good man," Fellows said. "And smart. He probably would've had something smarter to say to you than I have."

"You've done fine, Fred," Clint said, "just fine."

Fellows left Clint's hotel and walked over to the office of the *Yuma Daily Sun*. He walked in, ignored the noise of the press, and entered Steve Wynn's office. Before they spoke, Wynn pulled the shades down on all the windows.

"He's leaving today," Fellows said to him.

"I'm curious," the editor said. "Why didn't you take him to Joe Hickey yourself?"

"Because he didn't tell me that's why he was here," Fellows said. "And besides, you needed something for your paper, right? That interview?"

"It's going to run tomorrow."

"That's fine."

"Fred, what do you think he's going to find out there?"

"I don't know," Fellows said. "We won't know until he goes."

"Or until he comes back," Wynn said. "Maybe he'll come back with another story for me."

"Maybe," Fellows said. "I'll talk to you later."

"Where are you going?"

"I've got one more person to talk to."

Fellows found Mike Callum in the Red Bear Saloon. He was nursing a beer, rather than his usual bottle of whiskey. The deputy sat down opposite him.

"Callum."

Callum looked up at Fellows from his beer.

"What do you want, Deputy?"

"I've got a message for you from Joe Hickey."

Callum sat back so quickly his chair scooted across the floor. He put his hand on his gun.

"Relax, Callum," Fellows said. "I'm not gonna throw down on you. Just a warning."

"Yeah? What's the warning?"

"Lay off Clint Adams until he comes back to Yuma," Fellows said. "Once he comes back, you can do whatever you want."

"Or else?"

"I didn't say that, did I?"

"Does the sheriff know you're deliverin' messages for Joe Hickey?"

"That doesn't matter," Fellows said, standing up. "What matters is that it got delivered."

Fellows left the saloon. Callum sat at his table quietly for a few moments, then looked over at the bartender and yelled, "Whiskey!"

TWENTY-SEVEN

Clint collected Eclipse from the liveryman, whose face revealed how sad he was to see the big Darley Arabian go.

"Remember," he said, more to the horse than the man, "you promised to come back."

Clint rode out of Yuma and headed south, mindful of his back trail. After ten miles he decided he either was not being followed or was being followed by someone who was too good to be spotted.

Since he'd left Yuma after nine a.m., the general store had been open, and he had outfitted himself as he usually did, lightly. Coffee and beef jerky. He camped the first night, built a fire, and dined on his meager stores. He figured he'd eaten well enough in Yuma to be able to keep himself going on the coffee and jerky for a few days. He remembered the days he'd travel around with his gunsmithing wagon, which could be filled with more supplies than he ever would have needed. He ate well during those days, but covered a lot less ground.

He rolled himself into his bedroll eventually, secure in the knowledge that Eclipse would react if anyone came near the camp.

The next morning he finished the coffee that was left in the pot from the night before, then started following Joe Hickey's map again. Hickey had made sure to mark the map clearly, so Clint would not be as surprised by the appearance of Organ Pipe in front of him—or the site where Organ Pipe had once stood.

Continuing southwest, Clint checked the map to see if Hickey had indicated how far from Mexico Organ Pipe actually was. He had. It was almost on the border. He wondered if there were any Mexican towns nearby that might have been affected—or actually infected.

Had the sickness started with livestock and moved on to people?

He wondered if there'd be a dearth of animals as he got closer, but that didn't seem to happen. He saw bugs, birds, and mammals in abundance. If there was any remnant of disease present, he was sure that wouldn't have been the case.

Clint was surprised to find himself approaching the end of the trip—according to the map—before nightfall. If he pushed it, he could get there without having to make camp, but he decided he didn't want to do that. He would rather ride into the site in daylight.

He reined Eclipse in and made camp.

* * *

It took one day for Mike Callum to change his mind. One day, and several bottles of whiskey, and he decided he wasn't afraid of Joe Hickey, or Fred Fellows for that matter.

Early the morning after Clint Adams left, Callum saddled his horse and rode out of Yuma, heading southwest. Or as near to southwest as he could figure while being drunk.

By the time he camped that night, he had fallen off his horse several times, and when he sobered up sitting at his fire, he realized he hadn't brought any supplies with him. Except for one thing he had in his saddlebags at all times.

A bottle of whiskey.

He went to sleep in his bedroll with a smile on his face.

Eclipse woke Clint in the morning. Clint was instantly on his feet and alert.

"What is it, big boy?" he asked. "Somebody coming?"

Eclipse pawed the ground.

Clint turned, lifted his chin, and listened. He could hear it—hooves hitting the ground, and something else.

A bell?

The sound was coming closer, but slowly. Clint decided to put on a pot of coffee. By the time it was ready, the tinkling of the bell was right upon them.

A man, riding a donkey. No, a mule. He wasn't wearing a gun, but was wearing a bandolier for the rifle he was carrying.

"Hello, friend," the man said.

"Good morning."

"I smell coffee."

"It's just about ready," Clint said.

"Mind if I step down?" the man asked. "Never like to enter a man's camp without permission."

Clint picked up the coffeepot and said, "Sure. Permission granted, Mr.—"

"My name is Arnold," the man said, stepping down from the mule, "and this is Matilda."

TWENTY-EIGHT

Arnold had some beans in his pack, and a pan, but he had run out of coffee days ago, so they pooled their resources and had some breakfast.

"Ah," the older man said, "you know how to make trail coffee, my friend. I, uh, didn't catch your name."

"Clint."

Arnold's face was wrinkled where it wasn't covered by white hair—wrinkled and leathered. His eyes, though, they were a sparkling blue, a startling blue for a man so old. They were filled with life.

"Well, thanks for the coffee, Clint."

Clint handed Arnold a plate of beans and said, "Thanks for the grub."

"Beans ain't much to be thankful for," Arnold said, "but they fill the belly."

"All I had all day yesterday was beef jerky."

"Beef? Got any left?"

"Sure."

"Matilda loves beef."

"You want to give jerky to the mule?"

"Sure," Arnold said, walking over to her. "She's gotta eat, too, ya know."

"I suppose."

Arnold gave Matilda a nice big hunk of jerky, then came back to the fire to finish his coffee and beans.

"That's some animal you got there," he said. "He got a name?"

"Eclipse."

"Good name," Arnold said. "Strong. Where are you and Eclipse headed?"

"Organ Pipe."

Arnold stopped chewing and stared.

"Organ Pipe? Why the hell would you wanna go there?" he asked.

"I got a message from somebody," Clint said. "Somebody who needed help."

"What kind of message?"

"Came on the wind," Clint said.

"Well, that's some kinda message to get," Arnold said, chewing and washing the mouthful down with coffee.

"You from around here?"

"Friend Clint," Arnold said, "that's all I do is travel around here—here and Mexico, maybe. Right now I'm huntin'."

"Huntin' what?"

"A wolf."

"Mexican wolf?" Clint asked.

"Big gray sucker," Arnold said. "You ain't seen 'im, have ya?"

"No."

"If ya do, do me a favor and leave 'im be," Arnold said. "He's kinda mine."

"Sure thing," Clint said. "Far be it from me to kill another man's wolf."

"So," Arnold asked, "who was this message from?"

"Don't know."

"And what kind of trouble were they in?"

"Don't know."

"And when was the message sent?"

"Don't know that either."

"Don't sound like you know much about this, friend Clint," Arnold said. "What if you're ridin' into a whole mess of trouble?"

"I'll know that when the time comes."

"Guess you will."

"So," Clint asked, "what do you know about Organ Pipe, Arnold?"

Clint waited for the man to lie to him, but instead Arnold said, "Pretty much what everybody knows about Organ Pipe."

"And what's that?"

Arnold jerked his chin and said, "It lies over that way."

"Lies?"

Arnold shrugged. "What's left of it."

"So then what I heard," Clint asked, "about it being burned to the ground because of a plague of some kind? It's true?"

"As true as anythin' you hear."

"That's not a very clear response, Arnold."

"If you knew everythin' there was to know about Organ Pipe," Arnold asked, "you wouldn't be goin' there yerself for answers, now would ya?"

"I guess not."

"You'll find all your answers when ya get there, friend Clint," Arnold said.

He finished his coffee and beans, stood up, cleaned up his pan and his plates, and stowed them back in his saddlebags.

"Here," Clint said, handing him some beef jerky. "For you and Matilda."

"Thanks," Arnold said.

He mounted the mule, then looked down at Clint.

"You be careful, now."

"You, too," Clint said, "with that wolf."

"I'll get 'im," Arnold said. "I always get them. Adios."

Clint watched Arnold ride off due south, then saddled Eclipse and rode southwest, to Organ Pipe.

Or what was left of it.

TWENTY-NINE

Clint had put the map away, because the location of Organ Pipe was supposed to be just ahead of him. Just over a series of hills. That much had been confirmed by Arnold's jerk of the chin.

Just then a flock of birds flew overhead. He watched them until they were out of sight, and then they turned and came back.

He crossed paths with a Gila monster, and a snake.

A jackrabbit.

And then a Mexican wolf.

He reined in Eclipse as the wolf crossed their path. It watched him warily as it went north. Clint would have had a nice clear shot at it, but the wolf was not doing him any harm. Eclipse also knew that, for he stood still and relaxed. And besides, Clint had promised Arnold. The older man had gone south on his mule, though, and here was his wolf going north.

When the wolf was gone, Clint gave Eclipse his head and off they went again.

Suddenly, up ahead, Clint saw something. It looked like . . . a steeple.

A steeple?

The top of a building?

He topped the hill the steeple was rising above and looked down on a town.

A complete town.

Many buildings.

People walking and riding up and down the streets.

But there wasn't supposed to be a town here.

Not anymore.

Clint rode down the hill toward the town ahead of him, not sure what the hell was going on. Was this Organ Pipe? Was it another town? And if so, had it been erected on the same site?

He rode down the main street and became the object of everyone's attention. Apparently they didn't get many strangers in town. It wasn't a large town, and a lot of the buildings looked empty, but it certainly didn't have the feel of a dying town. Rather, it felt like a town that was growing.

This was nothing like what he had expected.

Under close scrutiny the entire way, Clint began to look for a likely spot to rein in. He finally decided on the sheriff's office. Along the way he never saw the name of the town above any of the businesses, so he still didn't know where he was.

Oddly, not all the buildings looked new. This did not

have the appearance of a town that had been built within the last two years. The sheriff's office, in fact, looked as if it had been around for decades.

He entered without knocking, and found himself inside a small, cramped, good old-fashioned sheriff's office, with all the comforts of home for a sheriff, including the potbellied stove.

A man wearing a badge was standing before a gun rack, holding a carbine and a rag. The metal of the rifle gleamed with oil.

"Help ya?" he asked.

He was fairly young for a sheriff, mid-thirties. He put the rifle back on the rack and laid down the rag, then turned to face Clint head-on. He wore a well-cared-for Colt on his right hip.

"I've got a question," Clint said. "Thought I'd ask the local law rather than just stop somebody on the street. Besides, they all seem to be staring at me funny."

"What's the question?"

"Where am I?"

"Come again?"

"What's the name of this town?"

"You don't know where you are, friend?"

"If I did, I wouldn't be asking," Clint said.

"You lose your memory or somethin'?" the lawman asked. "Hit your head?"

"Nothing like that," Clint said. "I just didn't see any signposts, and none of the businesses have the name of the town on them."

"So you just want to know the name of the town?" the sheriff asked. "That it?"

"That's about it."

"I got a question for you first."

"Go ahead."

"What's your name?"

"Clint Adams," Clint said. He could see the name scored a bull's-eye with the man. "Now can you answer mine?"

"Sure, friend, sure," the sheriff said. "You're in the town of Organ Pipe."

THIRTY

"Are you sure?" Clint asked.

"Now, what kind of fool question is that?" the lawman asked. "Of course I'm sure."

"No, sorry—look, that's not what I meant," Clint said, "but all the information I've gotten about Organ Pipe lately is that it was burned to the ground because of some kind of plague."

The sheriff put both hands on the front of his gun belt. Clint had a feeling the man could get to his Colt just fine if he had a mind to.

"Where'd you hear that?"

"Around."

"And to hear it, you must've been askin' questions," the sheriff said.

"That's right."

"Why?" the man asked. "What's your interest in Organ Pipe?"

"What's your name?"

"Patterson," the man said, "Sheriff Harry Patterson."

"How long have you been sheriff?" Clint asked.

"Long enough," the lawman said.

"How long has this town been here?" Clint asked.

"A couple of years, maybe less."

"You got a newspaper here?"

"Sure."

"Called the *Organ Pipe Register*?"

The sheriff frowned.

"What's all this to you, Adams?" he asked. "What's the Gunsmith's interest in Organ Pipe?"

"I got a message saying somebody here needed help," Clint said.

"Message from who?"

"I don't know."

"And you came running?" the sheriff asked. "Because you got a message from somebody you don't know?"

"It's become a bad habit," Clint said.

"Bad habits can be hard to break."

"Don't I know it."

"Look," Clint said, "something's going on here. I don't know what, but I intend to find out."

"What makes you think somethin's wrong?" Patterson asked.

"Can I have a seat?" Clint asked.

"Be my guest."

The sheriff relaxed for the first time since Clint entered the office, and sat down.

Clint took the newspaper clipping from his pocket

and handed it to the sheriff across his desk. The man took it and looked at both sides.

"This is what brought you here?" he asked. "A scribble on an old newspaper?"

"Is that from your town newspaper?"

"Looks like it."

"It's dated over two years ago."

The sheriff looked at it again. "When did you get this?"

"Not long ago," Clint said. "It came into my camp on the wind."

"Blowing on the wind, you mean? It could've been blowing around Arizona for a long time."

"I know it."

"Why would you respond to somethin' like this?" Patterson asked. "Don't you have other things in your life to keep you busy?"

"Not at the moment," Clint said. "It started out as curiosity, but then people started lying to me about Organ Pipe, until I talked with a convict at Yuma Prison named Joe Hickey."

"Hickey?" The sheriff sat up. "You talked to Joe Hickey?"

"That's right."

"He's in Yuma?"

"Right again."

"Son of a bitch!"

"You know him?"

"Oh, I know him," Patterson said. "I know him real well."

"Well, he's the one who told me Organ Pipe was burned to the ground because of a plague."

"A plague?" Patterson laughed.

"You find that funny?"

"You got your horse outside?"

"That's right."

"Come with me," Patterson said. He stood up and grabbed his hat, headed for the door.

"Where we going?" Clint asked, standing and falling into step with the lawman.

"First to the livery to get my horse," Sheriff Patterson said, "and then I'm gonna show you somethin', Mr. Adams."

THIRTY-ONE

The ride took about three hours. Clint never asked Sheriff Patterson where they were going, because he had an idea. Finally, they came to the site of what looked like an old fire. It covered enough acreage to have been an entire town.

"Organ Pipe?" Clint asked.

"The original town of Organ Pipe," Patterson said. "This is where it stood."

"What happened?"

"I'll tell you what happened," Patterson said. "That is, I'll tell you what I think happened, but I can't prove it."

"Okay."

"Joe Hickey burned it to the ground," Patterson said. "Hickey and his men."

"How many men?"

"Four. Five. I'm not sure."

"Why?"

"You'd have to ask Hickey that," Patterson said. "The Joe Hickey I know might have done it just for fun."

"And his men? Why would they have done it?"

"Because he told them to."

"Were they that loyal to him?"

"They were that frightened of him," Patterson said, "as was the rest of the town."

"Were you sheriff then?"

"No."

"Who was?"

"A man named Bockwinkle."

"The man who is now the sheriff of Yuma?"

"That's right."

"Why isn't he the sheriff of the new Organ Pipe?" Clint asked.

"He didn't stay around," Patterson said, "didn't think Organ Pipe could be rebuilt."

"Well, it wasn't rebuilt, was it?" Clint asked. "You just named this other town Organ Pipe, right?"

"Wrong," Patterson said. "The people rebuilt their town. They just didn't want to do it here."

"Your Organ Pipe doesn't look all new."

"It isn't," Patterson said. "There were some buildings there already, but they'd been abandoned. The people decided that an abandoned town was a good head start, so they built on that site."

"Your Organ Pipe doesn't look fully populated, either."

Patterson explained, "We're still working on that."

"What about all the people from this Organ Pipe?" Clint asked.

"A lot of them moved on rather than rebuild."

"Why?"

"You'd have to ask them," Patterson said. "My guess is they thought Joe Hickey might come back."

"You knew Hickey, and suspected him of burning down the town," Clint said. "Why didn't you go after him?"

"I wasn't the sheriff then."

"Deputy?"

"No," Patterson said, "I wasn't wearin' a badge. I was . . . a merchant."

"How'd you get to be sheriff?"

"Somebody had to take the job once we rebuilt," Patterson said. "I came forward and the town council hired me."

"Why didn't the people just rebuild the town right here?"

"They took a vote, decided to move west," Patterson said. "Too many bad memories here."

Clint scanned the site with his eyes. The buildings had almost all been burned to the ground. The remnants were black, and so was the ground around them.

"Looks like a pretty intense fire."

"It was," Patterson said. "It was a dry season, the town went up like a tinderbox."

"Any fatalities?"

"Some."

"So Hickey and his men committed murder."

"That's right."

"Did Sheriff Bockwinkle go after them?"

"No."

"Why not?"

"He said he had no proof they did it."

"So he didn't share your theory?"

"My knowledge," Patterson said, "and no, he didn't share it."

"So let me get this straight, Sheriff," Clint said. "You're telling me that the burning of Organ Pipe had nothing do with a disease of any kind?"

"That's what I'm tellin' you."

"So why was that message written?"

Patterson shrugged.

"You'll have to find the person who wrote it, and ask them yourself."

THIRTY-TWO

They rode back to Organ Pipe, got there just before dusk.

"You gonna stay awhile?" Sheriff Patterson asked at the livery.

"Overnight, for sure," Clint said, "maybe a day or two after that."

"What for?"

"Like you said," Clint answered, "to find out for myself."

They put their horses up at the livery, and the sheriff walked Clint back to his office.

"Hotel down the street is nice," he said. "Quiet. In fact, the whole town is quiet, and I'd like to keep it that way."

"Why do you think Joe Hickey told me that Organ Pipe had been burned because of a disease?"

Patterson shrugged.

"I'm sure he wouldn't want to admit that he burned it down just to see it burn."

"And you don't know who any of his other men were?" Clint asked.

"I know a couple he used to hang around with," the sheriff said, "but I can't say they were with him when he burned the town down."

"What were their names?" Clint asked. "The ones you know about."

"Charlie Cross and Dick Lawford."

"Where are they now?"

"Far as I know," Patterson said, "they're dead."

"How'd they die?"

"They were killed in separate robbery attempts last year," the lawman said. "At least, that's what I heard."

Clint was carrying his saddlebags and rifle.

"I'm going to go get a room and leave my gear. Where's a good place to eat?"

"Right across the street from the hotel," Patterson said. "Best restaurant in town."

"Thanks."

"Do me a favor, will you?" Patterson asked.

"Yeah?"

"Let me know when you decide to leave town."

"I'll do that, Sheriff," Clint said.

The hotel was small and clean, with no dining room, but that was okay. Clint left his things in the room and went across the street to the restaurant recommended by the sheriff. Not only was the food good, but it was served to him by a lovely waitress in her thirties who had a sunny personality. He wondered if she was new to Organ Pipe, or if she was one of the citizens who had stayed to re-build the town.

He was thinking steak as he entered, but the wait-ress's suggestion and the smell changed his mind and he went with the special of the day, beef stew.

He drank coffee with his food, and afterward had more coffee with a slice of peach pie.

"Don't get too many people askin' for peach," the waitress said. "Usually apple, or sometimes rhubarb, but we keep peach on hand for special people."

She gave him a hint as to how special she thought he was by bumping him with a firm hip. He could feel the heat emanating from her body right through her apron.

It was dark out by the time he finished his supper.

"Just get into town today?" the waitress asked him.

"That's right," he said. "I'm staying at the hotel across the street."

"Business or pleasure?" she asked.

"Somewhere in between, I guess."

"Oh, a mystery man," she said, with a big smile. "I like mysteries."

"You do?"

She nodded.

"This town is sort of a mystery to me."

"Really? Why?"

"Well, I remember a town called Organ Pipe, but it wasn't here. It was farther . . . east."

"That was the old Organ Pipe," she said. "This is the new Organ Pipe."

"What happened to the old one?"

"Oh, it burned down."

"Really? When?"

"A couple of years ago."

"What happened?"

She lowered her voice and said, "Well, nobody really knows the whole story, but—"

"Rachel!"

She cringed, then turned and looked at the man standing in the kitchen doorway.

"You got work to do, girl," the man said.

He wasn't just standing in the doorway, he filled it. Well over six feet, and almost that wide, he had black, wiry hair on his arms, which, assuming he was the cook, Clint was glad he had not found on his plate.

"I gotta go, mister," Rachel said.

"Clint," he said, "my name's Clint. Maybe I'll see you later."

She smiled and said, "Yeah, maybe."

Clint got up to leave, and the big cook stared at him the whole way to the door.

THIRTY-THREE

Clint went to his room to read and wait. If he was any hand at reading women, he figured the waitress, Rachel, would be at his door as soon as she could. She was interested in him, and he was interested in her; only his interest was twofold: He wanted to see what she looked like without her apron, and he wanted to talk to her some more about "old" Organ Pipe.

He was sitting on the bed reading Mark Twain when a knock came at the door. It was soft, and gave every indication of being a woman's knock, but he took his gun to the door with him anyway.

It was Rachel. She smelled of beef stew and pie, not a bad combination.

Shyly, she asked, "Was I predictable?"

"Not at all," he said. "Come in."

"So you weren't waitin' for me?" she asked, as he closed the door.

"Well," he said, turning to face her, "I was hoping. I

mean," he showed her the gun, "would I be holding this
if I'd thought it was you?"

She seemed pleased that she hadn't been too
predictable—even if he was lying.

He holstered his gun on the bed rail and turned to
face her again. He could smell her beneath the cooking
smells, which excited him even more.

"I probably should've went home and took a bath
first," she said, suddenly uncomfortable.

"I don't think so," he said, moving closer to her. She'd
removed her apron, but was wearing the same cotton
dress. She was buxom, with clear white skin and long
dark hair. Her skin betrayed her job, since she didn't
spend much time out in the sun.

He took her by the shoulders, pulled her to him, and
kissed her. Her lips were tentative at first, then softened
and became responsive. He wrapped his arms around her,
pulling her to him tighter so that her full breasts were
crushed against his chest.

"I—I don't do this all the time, you know," she said,
pressing her head to his chest. "Go to the rooms of
strange men."

"I told you my name," he said. "That means I'm not a
strange man."

"Clint," she said, to prove she remembered.

"That's right," he said, pressing his lips to her soft
neck, "and you're Rachel."

"Oh my . . ." she said. She shivered as he kissed her
neck.

Slowly, he began to undo the buttons on the back of
her dress. When he had more of her skin bare, he ran his

fingertips over it and she shivered again. She stepped back long enough for him to remove the dress all the way and peel her undies from her so that she was naked. Her breasts were full, with rounded, heavy undersides, dark brown nipples, and just the a slightest hint of sag. He cupped them in his palms and flicked at the nipples with his thumbs.

"Who was the big mean-looking guy in the restaurant?" he asked.

"Who, Andy? He's just the cook. And the owner."

"Not your boyfriend?"

"No," she said, closing her eyes as he squeezed her breasts, "not my boyfriend. I—I don't h-have a boyfriend."

"That's good," he said, pressing his lips to the upper slopes of her breasts. "So there's nobody waiting for you at home?"

"No," she said, in a breathy voice, "I live by myself."

He lifted her breasts and touched the tip of his tongue to her nipples. He flicked then easily, then took them into his mouth and sucked them hard.

"Clint?"

"Yes?"

"It's been a long time for me," she said. "Can we make this last? I—I don't know when the next time will be."

"Well," he said, "as far as I'm concerned, the next time won't be long after this time. I mean, we have all night, right?"

"Yes, but . . . I mean after tonight," she said. "The men in this town . . . Well, there don't seem to be many real men in this town."

"That's too bad," he said, going to his knees in front of her. He pressed his mouth to her belly. "A woman like you deserves a real man."

"Ooh," she said, grabbing his head as he tongued her deep belly button. And then she said, "Oh," as he cupped her pubic mound with his right hand. She had a lot of hair there, which he liked. He probed it gently until the end of his middle finger found her very wet.

"Oh . . . my . . . God . . ." she said, as he dipped his finger into her gently.

THIRTY-FOUR

Andy Crawford closed the restaurant door, locked it, and walked to the sheriff's office. As he entered, Sheriff Patterson looked up from his desk.

"You don't look happy, Andy," he said.

"I ain't," Andy said. "There was a stranger sniffing around Rachel today."

"So?"

"He was askin' about the old Organ Pipe burnin' down," the cook said.

"That must be Clint Adams," Patterson said.

"You know about him?"

"Sure. I sent him over to you. Thought you could use the business."

"You sent him— Wait a minute," Andy said, suddenly. "Did you say Clint Adams?"

"That's right."

"The Gunsmith."

"Still right, Andy."

"What the hell is he doin' in town?" Andy asked. "And how did he find us?"

"It appears Joe Hickey drew him a map."

"Hickey!"

"Sit down before you explode, Andy," Harry Patterson said. "Yeah, it seems Hickey's in Yuma Prison."

"That's where he belongs, if you ask me," Andy said. "I hope they're plannin' on hangin' him."

"Did he spend money in your place?"

"Huh?"

"Adams, did he spend money in your place?"

"Oh, yeah, he ate. Beef stew."

"So you got any other problems?"

"I tol' you, he was sniffing around Rachel."

"Andy, all men sniff around Rachel," Patterson said. "She never gives any of 'em a tumble, including me."

"She better not."

"Andy, you act like she belongs to you," Patterson said. "She doesn't give you a tumble, either."

"Don't you worry," the big man said. "She'll marry me. I'll wear 'er down eventually."

"Well, I hope you do, Andy," Patterson said. "Anything else?"

"You gonna let Adams find out what really happened?" the cook asked.

"I don't know if that's up to me, Andy," Patterson said. "Why don't we wait and see?"

Andy stood up. "I was you, I'd run him outta town."

"Well, I guess that's why I'm the sheriff and you're the cook, Andy."

"I own my place!" Andy reminded him.

"Right, right," Patterson said. "Sorry, Andy. No offense meant."

"Hmph," Andy said, and huffed out of the office.

Patterson wondered if Rachel would ever give the man a tumble while he smelled of onions.

Clint moved his hands around to cup Rachel's chunky buttocks and pressed his face to her fragrant mound. She smelled a little bit of sweat, and a bath would have taken care of that, but she also smelled like a woman in heat. He wouldn't have traded that for the smell of any soap in the world.

He breathed on her mound, then probed through the hair with his tongue until he tasted her. She jumped, and her knees almost buckled as he licked her.

"Oooh, God, I gotta lie down!" she said, anxiously. "Or I'll fall down."

"Well," he said, "we wouldn't want you to fall down, and I plan on doing this for a while, so . . ."

He stood up, took her hand, and led her to the bed. He'd been lying on top of the sheet and blanket, so he pulled them down and then laid her gently on her back. He undressed slowly, while she watched, and as his rigid, straining cock came into view, her eyes widened and she reached for it.

She wrapped her hand around it, stroked it, leaned over and rubbed the smooth skin of it over her face. She did it so lovingly that he said, "Wow, it *has* been a while for you."

"Oh, that doesn't matter," she said. "You are the most beautiful man I've ever seen. This thing is just . . . well, beautiful."

She stroked it with both hands, then put her lips to it. Slowly, she opened her lips to let him slide inside. The interior of her mouth was wet and incredibly hot.

"Now I'm the one who has to lie down," he said as she sucked him.

She let him bob free of her mouth, laughed, then scooted over and said, "Get into this bed with me, you beautiful man!"

THIRTY-FIVE

Sheriff Harry Patterson swiveled his desk chair around, looked up at the gun rack, and reminded himself what he had been doing when Clint Adams first entered his office.

He took the carbine down, picked up his rag, located his gun oil, and continued to clean the weapon. Idly, he thought about Clint Adams's arrival in Organ Pipe and what it could mean to the town. He decided that early in the morning he'd go over and talk to the owner and editor of the *Register*, Paul Harris. Just as Patterson had not been the sheriff of Organ Pipe before the burning, Harris had not been the owner-editor of the *Register*. But they were here now, and between them they were the caretakers of the town. He had to warn—or, at least, advise—Harris that Clint Adams might be coming in to talk with him. After all, Patterson doubted that Adams had gotten all the answers he was looking for, and he doubted the man would ride back to Yuma without them.

* * *

Mike Callum rode into Organ Pipe in the dark, so no one could see him. He'd followed Clint Adams's trail there, but hadn't expected to find a town—not here, anyway. The Organ Pipe he had known was farther east.

This town was strange to him, but it was a town, and Clint Adams was here. He confirmed that when he stopped at the livery to put up his horse for the night. Had to wake the liveryman up, paid him double to open the doors, but there in a stall was Adams's big black.

"You know the man belongs to that horse?" he asked.

"Sure thing. Mr. Adams."

"Know where he's stayin'?"

"Hotel over on Main Street."

"Hotel got a name?"

"Nope," the man said, "just the hotel. Only one in town."

"Anyplace else to stay?"

"Yeah, a rooming house the other side of town. Run by a widder woman named Hastings."

"Thanks."

"You gonna leave yer horse here long?"

"I'll have to let you know," Callum said, and left to go and find that rooming house.

Andy left the sheriff's office and went over to the small house Rachel lived in, over near Mrs. Hastings's rooming house. There were no lights inside, and when he looked in the windows he couldn't see anything.

Goddamn woman.

Goddamn *whore*!

.

* * *

Clint had to wrestle with Rachel for who would be on top, and his superior strength prevailed.

"Isn't there some way we can do this together?" she complained.

"Not unless we invent one," he said.

"Oooh," she growled, "why do you like it so much down there?"

"I think," he said, and paused, "it might be because you taste a little like the daily special."

She started to laugh then, unable to stop even when tears began to roll down her face. Then, as he slid his hands beneath her to cup her buttocks and lift her, she suddenly stopped, because he had new and better access to her. He licked and sucked on her avidly until she was growling again, but for a different reason. She was bucking beneath him, reaching for something she'd never expected because she'd never experienced it before.

He ran his hands over her big breasts, meaty thighs, soft belly, continuing to work on her with his mouth until her body went taut and she screamed . . .

She was curled up on the bed, trying to catch her breath, holding her hand out as if to hold him at bay.

"W-what was t-that?" she asked, breathlessly.

"You've never felt that before?" he asked.

"No," she said, "never. Does that happen . . . all the time with you?"

"Well, not with me, but with a lot of the women I'm with," he said.

"Jesus!" she said. "I guess I've just never been with the right man before."

"I'm flattered."

"I thought I was gonna die," she said. "It was so damn good I thought I was gonna die."

"Well," Clint said, "you're not going to die, and we're not done."

"God," she said, fervently, "I hope not!"

THIRTY-SIX

By morning Rachel was determined that Clint was never going to leave Organ Pipe.

"The first time it happened, I thought it was a fluke," she admitted, "but every time? Jesus, now all you have to do is touch me and I explode. That's what it feels like, you know. An explosion. What will I do after you leave? You have ruined me for every other man I'll ever meet."

"I'm sure you'll find another man you can feel the same way with," he said.

"No," she said, "huh-uh, I don't think so. I'm thirty-eight years old, Clint, and you're the first man I've ever met who can do that to me. My God, I've had sex hundreds of times! Never . . . never . . . no," she said, starting to stammer, "I don't think—I mean, this was a once-in-a-lifetime thing."

"Rachel, you don't have to—"

"Can we do it again?"

It was morning; he was hungry, and he wanted to go and see the editor of the newspaper.

"Now?" he asked.

"Right now," she said, reaching for his cock. "Look, you're getting hard already—again. That's another thing. All the other men I've ever been with grunt over me and then roll over and go to sleep. I've never been with a man who can do it so many times."

"It's not me," he said, "it's you, Rachel. You're so beautiful, and you have a wonderful body, and you're so damn—"

"Stop!" she said, putting her hands over her ears.

"Why?"

"Nobody's ever talked to me that way before," she said. "Maybe I've just been living in little towns too long. Men like you don't come along every day, Clint, do you know that?"

"Come here," he said, reaching for her.

She went into his arms willingly, anxiously. They rolled over on the bed and she climbed on top of him. She reached between them to find him fully hard already. She lifted her hips, held him, and sat down on him, taking him inside.

"Oh my God," she said, as she rode him up and down, "oh my God, oh my God, oh . . . my . . . God!"

Paul Harris, owner and editor of the *Organ Pipe Register*, looked up from his printing press as Sheriff Harry Patterson walked in. The press wasn't running, which was why Harris happened to be bent over it at the moment.

"Can't get the damned thing to run," Harris said, straightening up. "What can I do for you, Harry?"

"We gotta talk."

"About what?"

"Fella in town askin' questions about the old town."

"So?"

"Fella's name is Clint Adams."

Harris picked up a rag and wiped his hands on it, stepped away from the press.

"Well, that sounds more interesting than what I'm doing," he said. "Come on, have a cup of coffee and tell me all about it."

Clint went to breakfast alone. Rachel had finally succumbed to exhaustion and remained in his bed. He told her to stay there as long as she wanted, and she asked if forever would be too long.

Since Rachel was in his bed, he didn't go to her restaurant for breakfast. He found another place, smaller, not crowded, where the man who was the cook was also the waiter—and probably the owner. But the food was pretty good.

"Why was I told that the other restaurant was the best one in town?" Clint asked the man. "The place across from the hotel?"

"I don't know," the man said, frowning. He was the opposite of Andy, the other cook. This man was about five and a half feet tall, with slate gray hair but with a black mustache. "Who told you that?"

"Oh, I don't know," Clint said. "I just heard it . . . around."

"Well, what do you think?" the man asked. "Now that you ate in both places?"

"Well," Clint said, "I had beef stew there and eggs here. Kind of hard to compare those. But I can tell you one thing."

"What's that?"

"Your coffee's better."

The man stuck out his hand.

"Carl Crews."

"Cruz?" Clint asked, shaking his hand. "You don't look Mexican."

"Not," Carl said. "It's Crews." And he spelled it out for Clint.

"Oh, I see. Well, my name's Clint Adams."

"The Gunsmith," Crews said. "In my place? More coffee?"

"Yeah," Clint said, "definitely."

Crews poured him another cup. By this time the other two diners had left.

"What brings you to town?" Crews asked.

"I was looking for Organ Pipe," Clint said. "The, uh, other one."

"Oh," Crews said.

"Did you live there?"

"No," Crews said. "I came here later."

"Did Andy live there?"

"Oh, yeah, he did."

"Maybe that explains it," Clint said. "Why folks eat there more than here?"

"I never looked at it that way, but you're probably right."

"Is there that kind of separation here?" Clint asked. "Folks from the old Organ Pipe and folks from the new one?"

"Oh yeah," Crews said. "In fact, I think that may be what's keepin' us from growin' as fast as we could."

"You mind talking to me about that, Mr. Crews?" Clint asked.

"Hell, I don't mind at all," Crews said. "Ain't every day I get to talk to the Gunsmith." Crews sat down. "What's on your mind?"

THIRTY-SEVEN

Paul Harris listened to Sheriff Patterson, then sat back in his chair and stared at the man.

"What the hell?" he said. "Where did this story of a plague come from?"

"Joe Hickey."

"Son of a bitch."

"I know."

"Hickey's been in Yuma all this time?" Harris asked.

"'Pears like."

"And who else is in Yuma?"

"Don't know," Patterson said.

"Well," Harris said, "somebody should ask Adams, don't you think?"

"He's comin' to see you next, probably," Patterson said.

"So I should ask him?"

"Why not?"

"I'm not the sheriff."

"Come on, Paul," Patterson said. "You and me, we're equal in this."

"Except you got to wear the badge, and I got to run the newspaper."

"You wanted to run the newspaper."

"Yeah, well . . . Okay, when he comes, I'll feel him out, talk to him," Harris said. "See what I can find out."

"Maybe get him on our side," Patterson said.

"I tell you what," Harris said. "I'll feel him out, find out what he knows . . . You get him on our side."

"Paul—"

"That feels more equal to me, Harry."

Patterson sighed. "Fine."

Because Crews felt like an outsider in the new Organ Pipe, Clint had the feeling he could trust him. He laid out his thoughts for the man, who listened carefully and waited until Clint was done before asking questions.

"And who told you about a plague?"

"Joe Hickey."

"Well, I don't know this Hickey," Crews said, "but that don't mean he wasn't part of the old Organ Pipe."

"And the plague?"

"I never heard nothin' about no plague," Crews said. "I heard a gang had Organ Pipe under their thumb, and when the town decided to fight back, the gang burned it down."

"That'd be Joe Hickey's gang."

"You better talk to the sheriff about that."

"I did," Clint said, "but I get the feeling I'm not getting the whole story."

"So what's your next move?"

"The newspaper."

"Paul Harris," Crews said.

"He the editor?"

"Editor, owner, reporter—he does it all," Crews said. "Usually up to his elbows in printing press ink, trying to get the thing to keep workin'."

"So you know him?"

"He's old Organ Pipe, but yeah, I know 'im. Don't think you're gonna need me for an introduction, though."

"Why not?"

"Once you tell him who you are, he'll smell a story."

"Or an interview," Clint said, sourly.

"Probably."

"I've done enough interviews for one week," Clint said.

"Yuma?"

Clint nodded.

"Newspapermen," Crews said. "They think alike. You could probably trade him an interview for some information, though."

"That's what I did in Yuma."

"Was it worth it?"

"Got me to Joe Hickey."

"And that got you here," Crews said. "Seems like you've come as far as you can on that bargain. Might be time to make another one."

"Might be."

A young couple walked in the front door, and Crews said, "Glory be, I got more customers."

"Go take care of them," Clint said. "Thanks for listening, Carl."

"Sure thing," Crews said, standing up. "Lemme know what happens, will ya?"

"I'll do that."

Clint went past the young couple, who were new in town and looking for a good breakfast.

"You're in for a treat," Clint said. "Good breakfast here."

"Thank you, sir," the young woman said, with a smile.

Her husband scowled at Clint and put his arm around his young bride protectively.

Clint left and headed for the newspaper office.

THIRTY-EIGHT

"Clint Adams?" Paul Harris asked as Clint entered the newspaper office.

"How'd you guess?"

"I was told you'd be comin' to see me."

"Told, or warned?"

"Both, I guess," Harris said. "What's the difference? Paul Harris." He wiped his hand on a rag and then extended it to be shaken. "Don't worry. It's just a little ink."

Clint shook the man's hand. A negligible amount of ink was transferred.

"Why don't we go into my office and have a drink?" Harris said.

"Fine."

He led the way down a hallway and into a small room.

"This was one of the buildings left standing here," he said, getting a bottle out of the bottom drawer of a roll-top desk. "I decided to renovate it, rather than build a new one."

He pulled out two coffee mugs, poured two fingers of whiskey into each, and handed Clint one. There were two chairs in the room. He sat at the one in front of his desk.

"Have a seat."

Clint took the remaining chair.

"I heard you'd have some questions for me."

Clint took the clipping from his pocket and passed it over.

"This what brought you here?"

"That's right."

Harris studied it.

"Before my time, from the old Organ Pipe," he said. "According to the date, anyway. Who wrote this on it?"

"I don't know," Clint said. "Don't think I'll ever find out."

"But you came anyway?"

Clint took the clipping back. "Somebody needed help."

"That was probably written while Joe Hickey and his gang were in control of Organ Pipe."

"Sounds likely. Who else was in Hickey's gang?"

"Why do you want to know that?"

"So I can talk to them."

"The sheriff told me you came here from Yuma," Harris said.

"That's right."

"And that Joe Hickey's in prison there?"

"Right again."

"Well, if Joe Hickey was in Yuma, I'll bet some of his gang is still there. I'll bet you've already talked to them."

"I won't know that until somebody gives me some names," Clint said. "Nobody's being very forthcoming about Organ Pipe's history."

"Well," Harris said, "a lot of us are not proud of the town's history."

"And why's that?"

"Because we stood by and let Joe Hickey bully us," Harris said.

"What was your job in the old Organ Pipe?"

"I was a clerk at a store," Harris said. "But I wanted to be a newspaperman."

"Why didn't you work at the newspaper?"

"The editor wouldn't hire me."

"Why not?"

"He was a friend of Joe Hickey's."

"Joe Hickey had friends?" Clint asked. "I thought he just had gang members."

"Some of the citizens became his friends. I guess they thought they'd get preferential treatment."

"They were sleeping with the enemy?"

"You could say that," Harris answered. "Eating and drinking with him, anyway."

"And you know the names of these citizens?"

"I know some," Harris said, "the sheriff knows some others. Why?"

"Well, folks have been lying to me, Mr. Harris," Clint said. "I'd kind of like to know why."

"You mean about the plague?"

"And I mean about not knowing a thing about a town called Organ Pipe."

"Well, maybe some of the gang is actually ashamed of what they did," Harris said.

"Mr. Harris," Clint said, "can you just give me some names?"

Harris poured himself more whiskey, offered Clint some. He shook his head.

"Just the names."

"Well, I don't know if you've met any of these gents or not," Harris said. "You might try talking to Fred Fellows, and Steve Wynn."

"What positions did they hold in Organ Pipe?"

"Fellows was a deputy, and Steve Wynn ran the paper."

"And they were friendly with Joe Hickey?"

"They made sure Hickey knew they weren't against him," Harris said.

"I've already run into Fellows and Wynn," Clint said. "In fact, it was Wynn who took me to see Hickey in prison."

"Are they in Yuma?"

"They most certainly are in Yuma," Clint said, "and doing much the same thing they did in Organ Pipe."

"Son of a bitch," Harris said. "I had no idea they were so close."

"Took a lot of nerve, I guess," Clint said.

"Have you run into Mike Callum yet?"

"Callum? No. Who is he?"

"He was one of Hickey's men. I heard he stays

close to Hickey. If you haven't run into him, you will, and I'd watch my back."

"I'll do that. Thanks for talking to me, Mr. Harris."

"Where are you off to now?"

"To see the sheriff," Clint said. "Reckon I can get the last of what I need from him."

"Good luck."

THIRTY-NINE

"Mike Callum?" Sheriff Patterson repeated. "Sure, I know him. He was part of the Hickey gang."

"So he helped Hickey burn the town down?"

"Sure."

"And those other two you told me about?"

"Yep."

"So now that you know that Callum is in Yuma, will you go and get him?"

"Nope."

"Why not?"

"I can't prove he and Hickey burned the town down," Patterson said.

"No witnesses?"

"Not witnesses that will come forward."

"What about Fellows and Wynn?"

"I don't like them," Patterson said, "but they didn't break the law. All they did was look out for themselves."

"Why do you think they went to Yuma, and didn't stay here and help you rebuild?"

"Nobody would've worked with them, or spoken to them," Patterson said. "They were traitors."

"So they wouldn't have gotten their jobs back?"

"Jobs. Lives." Patterson shrugged. "They wouldn't have been welcome here."

"Well, Yuma welcomed them."

"Nobody in Yuma knew what they did," Patterson said. "Course, if you went back to Yuma and told people . . ."

"But there's no proof, right?"

"You're not the law," Patterson said. "You're the Gunsmith. Why do you need proof?"

"I'm not just going to shoot someone," Clint said. "Not on your say-so, anyway."

Patterson shrugged again.

"As long as they don't come back here, I got no problem with them," Patterson said.

Clint nodded and stood up.

"Well, thanks for the information, anyway," Clint said. "At least I know why some people were lying to me."

"They got something to hide."

Clint started out, then stopped.

"You know a black man named Antoine? Got a young girl with him, named Jada?"

"Antoine ran the livery in Organ Pipe," Patterson said. "He ran out before the fire even started."

"Was he part of Hickey's gang?"

"Don't know," Patterson said. "He just lit out."

"Well," Clint said, "he's on the run from something."

"You headin' back to Yuma?" Patterson asked.

"Right now," Clint said. "I want to wrap this up and get back to my life."

"What about whoever wrote that note?"

"Don't think I ever expected to find that out," Clint said. "See ya, Sheriff."

"Probably not," Patterson said, as the door closed behind Clint.

Moments after Clint walked out, Patterson heard two shots. He sighed, got up, and headed for the door.

As Clint stepped outside, he saw a man in the street, facing him, maybe waiting for him.

"Saw you go in," the man said. "Figured I'd wait out here."

"Let me guess," Clint said. "Mike Callum."

"Gonna make a name for myself, Adams, by killin' you," Callum said, "no matter what Joe Hickey says."

"Going to make a name for yourself, all right," Clint said, "but it won't be for killing me. It'll be for getting killed by me."

"No more talk."

Clint shrugged. Callum went for his gun, but never made it.

FORTY

When Clint rode Eclipse back into the livery in Yuma, he made the liveryman very happy.

"You brought him back," he said, happily jumping from one foot to the other and back.

"Take good care of him," Clint said.

"Of course."

Clint had made one stop before coming back to the town. He'd stopped at the Yuma Territorial Prison . . .

"Back for another visit?" Warden Kelsey asked.

"If that's all right with you, Warden."

"Hey, it's all right with me if it's all right with Hickey," Kelsey said. "I'll just check."

Clint waited in the warden's office with a guard while Kelsey went to talk to Joe Hickey. When the warden came back, he said, "Come this way."

Kelsey walked Clint to the same room where he'd

met with Hickey before. Once again, the guard waited outside and Hickey was seated at the table, in chains.

"Glad to see you're okay," Hickey said. "Justifies my faith in you."

"You knew Callum was coming after me?"

"The idiot came to see me, told me he was gonna try you," Hickey said. "I tried to talk him out of it. I knew you'd kill him. You did kill him, didn't you?"

"I killed him," Clint said. "He gave me no choice."

"Course not."

"What about the others?" Clint asked. "Your other partners in burning down Organ Pipe?"

"Partners?" Hickey asked. "As far as I know, Callum was the last one, and now he's dead."

"But you're still in here, and your friends are out there."

"Friends?"

"You know," Clint said. "Deputy Fellows and the newspaper editor, Steve Wynn? Your friends from the old Organ Pipe?"

"How does it look?" Hickey asked.

"How does what look?"

"The new town," Hickey said. "How does the new Organ Pipe look?"

"It looks fine," Clint said. "Not that you're ever going to see it."

"So you went there, and you have the whole story, right?"

"Right," Clint said. "No disease, no plague, just a man who wanted to see a town burn."

"I was good to them," Hickey said. "Me and my boys, we kept those people safe, and what did they do? They turned on me."

"They wanted you out of their town."

"My town!" Hickey shouted. He tried to bring his fist down on the table, but the chains inhibited him, so he just kind of knocked on the tabletop. "It was my town."

"You owned it?"

"That's right."

"And since you owned it, you figured you had the right to burn it."

"Right again."

"Aren't you afraid of what might happen now that you're admitting it?"

"Admitting what?" Hickey asked. "There's only you and me here, Gunsmith. I'll just deny I ever said anything. Besides, what would they do, hang me twice?"

"I understand you're in here for something you didn't do."

"That's right," Hickey said. "Railroaded by that sheriff, his senior deputy, and the newspaperman."

"I understood Wynn was your benefactor."

"I don't know what that is."

"That he stood up for you? Argued for you in his newspaper."

"Oh yeah, he made it look real good, but they all lied to get me in here."

"The sheriff, too? What's his name? Bockwinkle?"

"Now, there's a man who may be hard to kill," Hickey said, "but I have faith that you'll get it done."

"I'm not killing a lawman, Hickey," Clint said.

"No, you ain't," Hickey said. "You're gonna kill two lawmen. And a newspaper editor."

"And why would I do that?"

"Because they ain't gonna give you a choice," Hickey said. "Now that you're back from Organ Pipe, you know the truth. You know they was all . . . what did they call 'em in the war . . . collaborators?"

"That's right." Clint said. "All of them? I heard about Fellows and Wynn. What did Bockwinkle do in Organ Pipe?"

"Nothin'," Hickey said. "He ain't from there, but he helped the other two put me in here."

"Why would he do that?"

"Why does anybody do anythin'?"

"Money?"

"You got it."

"Fellows and Wynn? Where'd they get enough money to buy a sheriff?"

"Nobody told you about the Organ Pipe bank?"

"No," Clint said, "nobody told me about the bank. You robbed it?"

"I took the blame for robbin' it," Hickey said, "but I never did. All I did was burn it down, with the rest of the town."

"You're saying Fellows and Wynn robbed the bank?"

"Why do you think they didn't go to the new Organ Pipe?" Hickey asked. "They came here instead, to start over."

"Why come here? Why so close to Organ Pipe?"

"Two reasons. One, nobody would look for them this

close. And two, if they did find them here, it wouldn't look like they ran, just relocated."

"Kind of does look like that," Clint admitted.

"Yeah, well, they relocated all right, with a bunch of money."

"Funny, nobody in Organ Pipe mentioned that to me."

"They don't trust nobody in Organ Pipe."

"You saw to that, didn't you?"

"Oh yeah . . ."

"I'm curious, Hickey."

"About what?"

"Why'd you send me to Organ Pipe? Why'd you tell me an idiotic story about a plague?"

"I figured you wouldn't be able to resist then," Hickey said. "And I wanted you to hear the whole story."

"So now you want me to take care of your three, uh, backers?"

"Why not? They deserve it. They deserve to be in here, not me."

"You deserve to be here just for burning down a town," Clint said.

"But that ain't what I'm in here for."

"Too bad," Clint said, standing up. "As far as I'm concerned, you deserve to be in here for what you did to that town."

"I call that not fair," Hickey said.

"I call it justice," Clint said.

FORTY-ONE

Clint didn't have any intention of killing Fred Fellows, Steve Wynn, and Nick Bockwinkle for Joe Hickey, but neither could he let them get away with robbing a bank, assisting in burning down a town, and, oh, yeah, trying to use him.

The first thing he had to do was let them know he was back. Then he'd let nature take its course.

He entered the sheriff's office, saw Deputy Fellows standing in front of the desk while a big-bellied man with a sheriff's badge sat behind it.

"Well, speak of the devil," Fellows said. "I was just talkin' about you, Adams."

"And here I am."

"Here you are," Fellows said, "back already. Did you find out what you needed to find out?"

"I found out everything, Deputy," Clint said. "Why don't you introduce me to your sheriff?"

"Sheriff Bockwinkle, this is Clint Adams, the Gunsmith."

Bockwinkle gave Clint a wary look, and did not rise or extend his hand.

"Is there gonna be trouble?" he asked.

Clint wasn't sure who the man was asking.

"If you're asking me, I'd say yes," Clint said. "If you're asking your deputy . . . well, I don't know. What do you think, Deputy? Is there going to be trouble?"

Fellows started to reply, but Clint cut him off.

"Before you answer that, you should know that I paid another visit to Joe Hickey."

"Why'd you do that?"

"To get the last pieces of the puzzle in place," Clint said.

"And did you?"

"I did, Deputy," Clint said. "I surely did. I'm going to go to my hotel now and get some rest, but I'll be seeing you later."

Clint walked to the door, then turned.

"Oh, and would you tell Steve Wynn I'm back?" he asked. "I'll want to talk to him."

As Clint went out the door, Fellows turned to Bockwinkle and gave him a look.

"To answer your question," Fellows said, "yeah, I think there's gonna be a lot of trouble."

FORTY-TWO

Bockwinkle and Fellows went to the offices of the *Yuma Daily Sun*. They told Steve Wynn that Clint was back and there was going to be trouble.

"Why did we ever think different?" Wynn asked. "Once he talked to Hickey—"

"You took him to talk to Hickey," Bockwinkle pointed out.

"He thought I should take him to Hickey," Wynn said, pointing to Fellows.

"Why did you think that, Fred?" Bockwinkle asked.

"I thought it would be better for him to get to Hickey through one of us than on his own."

"Yeah, but you made sure it was me, not you," Wynn said.

"What else have you made sure of, Fred?" Bockwinkle asked. "You know, you're a pretty smart fella."

"Look," Fellows said, "fighting among ourselves is just what Adams would want. We have to figure out what to do about him, because by now he knows the truth."

"About you two," Bockwinkle said. "There's no truth to know about me."

"Except that you're takin' money from us," Fellows said.

"And by now he knows it's Bank of Organ Pipe money," Wynn said.

Bockwinkle frowned.

"Okay," he said, "so Clint Adams, the famous Gunsmith, has to die in Yuma, Arizona. It'll put us on the map."

"And carrying the story will make my paper," Wynn said.

"I think when this is over," Fellows said, "I'll be leavin' Yuma. Yeah, I think I'm gonna settle down someplace quiet."

"Like Organ Pipe?" Bockwinkle asked.

"Very funny, Nick," Fellows said. "Listen, we've got to get those two idiot deputies of yours to kill Adams."

"Why them?" Bockwinkle asked.

"Because," Fellows said, "they can do it legally. All you've got to do is tell them that he's wanted and there's a reward, and they can have it if they bring him in—dead or alive."

"Will they do it?" Wynn asked.

"Of course they'll do it," Bockwinkle said. "They're a couple of idiots."

As they walked back to the sheriff's office, Fellows said, "You know we're gonna have to go with them, don't you?"

"I know," Bockwinkle said. "What about Wynn?"

"He's no good with a gun."

"Four to one, not bad odds," Bockwinkle said.

"Yeah," Fellows said. "Not bad."

Clint grabbed a straight-backed wooden chair from the hotel lobby, took it outside with him, and sat. They were going to have to come after him, or take the chance he would expose them. He wasn't doing this for Joe Hickey. Hickey was going to get his neck stretched eventually. No, this was for the people who lost everything when Organ Pipe burned down.

This was for whoever had sent him that message on the wind.

FORTY-THREE

"This is great!" Deputy Stone said, excitedly.

"Keep calm, boy," Bockwinkle said. "You get too excited, you're gonna end up dead."

"Are you sure about this, Sheriff?" asked Deputy Bennett.

"We're sure, Bennett," Fellows said. He handed each deputy a shotgun from the gun rack.

"We could probably use some more help," Bennett said. "What about Mike Callum? I could get—"

"I'm sure Callum's dead, Bennett," Fellows said. "I'm sure Adams killed him already."

"What's he done?" Stone asked. "Murder? Is it Mike Callum? Is that what we're bringin' him in for?"

"All you gotta know is this is your job, Stone," Bockwinkle said. "Stop askin' fool questions."

"How are we gonna do this?" Bennett asked.

Bockwinkle looked at Fellows.

"He'll concentrate on me, Fred," the sheriff said. "That'll give you an edge."

"Right."

"What about us?" Stone asked.

"Yeah, you, too," Bockwinkle said. "You'll have an edge."

"All right!"

Bennett did not look as excited or pleased as Stone did about bringing in Clint Adams.

From the front window of his office Steve Wynn had a clear view of the hotel. He could see Clint Adams sitting out front. Goddamn if he wasn't just waiting for them, looking just as calm and collected as you please.

If Adams managed to kill both Fellows and Bockwinkle, Wynn's plan was to go out the back door, and just keep on going. He still had enough of the Organ Pipe bank money to start over somewhere else.

He settled down to watch the show.

"You boys are gonna stand between me and Fellows," Bockwinkle instructed. "Understand?"

Bennett nodded and Stone said, "Sure."

Bockwinkle looked at Fellows.

"This is what it all comes down to," he said to his senior deputy.

"I know."

"Whataya talkin' about?" Stone asked.

"Never mind," Bockwinkle said. "It's time to go."

Fellows knew he could've got up on a rooftop with a rifle, but that would have been an ambush. In front of the whole town. They had to make it look legal, or it was all over for him in Yuma.

"I'm ready," he said.

Bockwinkle wished he had time to gather more men. But he'd been through this kind of thing before. As good as Adams was, maybe he wasn't as good as they said he was. Four men with guns, that was a big disadvantage. One of them might even plug him by accident. He'd seen it happen before. The Gunsmith was going to have to rush his shots, and there might even be some hesitation when he realized he was shooting at four badges.

Bockwinkle knew he just had to wait for that one weak moment, and hope it would come.

Clint took out his gun, checked it, and then holstered it. He could see the front of the newspaper office from his chair. He was sure Steve Wynn was at the window, looking out, waiting for the action. He was either going to write about it or run from it.

Clint had one problem with what was about to happen. He'd be facing men wearing badges—four of them, if Bockwinkle and Fellows brought the other two deputies. If they did that, it would be a shame. Deputies Stone and Bennett had no idea what they were getting involved with. It was Clint's hope that he'd be able to explain it to them, get them to step back from the action.

The other two, Bockwinkle and Fellows, their badges were tarnished. They didn't deserve to be wearing badges at all. Clint wondered if he'd be able to talk them into taking them off.

He saw them now, walking down the street carrying

shotguns. Four scatterguns could do a lot of damage, and some of that would be accidental.

He remained seated and calm as they approached. He hoped that the steady nerves would be on his side.

FORTY-FOUR

As the four "lawmen" stopped in front of the hotel, Clint could see the two deputies in the center sweating profusely.

"Hello, gents," he said, not moving from his chair.

"Time for you to come quietly, Adams," Bockwinkle said.

"On what charge?"

"Don't you worry about that," the sheriff said. "We'll take care of all that once you're in a nice cell."

"You know I'm not going to any cell, Sheriff," Clint said. He looked at the deputies. "You boys ready to die so the sheriff here can keep getting his payday from Fellows and Wynn?"

"Shut up, Adams!" Fellows said.

"What's he mean?" Bennett asked.

"Never mind," Fellows said. "Don't listen to him."

"You didn't know?" Clint asked. "Your sheriff is getting paid by your senior deputy and the newspaper editor. He's on the payroll, and they don't want me telling anyone about it."

"What's goin' on?" Stone asked, nervously.

"They're willing to sacrifice you to try to shut me up," Clint said. "You boys aren't going to make it out of today alive unless you turn around now and walk away."

Both men licked their lips and each exchanged a glance.

"Okay, Adams," Bockwinkle said. "It's time." He thumbed back the hammers on his shotgun.

Clint stood up, and both deputies flinched.

"Back off, Deputies," he said. "This is between your bosses and me. It doesn't even have anything to do with the badges."

Fellows thumbed back the hammers on his shotgun.

"You boys ready?" Fellows asked.

"Yeah," Clint said, "you boys ready to die?"

Both men bit their lips, exchanged another glance, and then Bennett took a step back. He was followed by Stone. Then another step. Then they both dropped their shotguns in the street and backed away, hands in the air.

"Now you, Sheriff," Clint said. "You want to die to cover up for what Fellows and Wynn did in Organ Pipe?"

Bockwinkle licked his lips, and from the corner of his eye Clint saw Fellows raise the barrel of the shotgun ever so slightly. Clint drew and fired. His shot took Fellows in the chest, just below the badge. The shotgun discharged into the air, and Clint heard some glass break above his head.

Fellows went down onto his back, and Clint turned the barrel of his gun to Bockwinkle.

"Hold it, hold it," the sheriff said. "Don't shoot."

"Drop the shotgun."

The man did as he was told.

Clint looked at the other two deputies, who were under the gun of Sheriff Harry Patterson of Organ Pipe. Clint had not seen where Patterson had come from.

"Thought I'd keep them honest for you," Patterson said.

"Much obliged, Sheriff," Clint said. "Glad you're here. This town's going to need a temporary lawman."

"Whataya mean   " Bockwinkle started, but Clint cut him off.

"All three of you," he said. "Drop your gun belts and then your badges—now!"

Stone and Bennett obeyed. Bockwinkle hesitated, then followed.

"You want to take them over to the jail?" Clint asked.

"Sure thing, Adams."

"I got one more visit to make."

As Clint hurried to the livery, he knew there'd be nothing to hold the two deputies on. They'd just been unlucky enough to be caught up in something they had no real part of.

Bockwinkle would lose his badge, maybe do some time. That would be up to a judge.

As Clint got to the livery, Steve Wynn was just about to mount his hastily saddled horse. There were two bulging saddlebags already in place.

"That's far enough, Wynn."

The editor stopped and turned. He was unarmed.

"Lemme go, Adams," he pleaded. "I'll leave one of these saddlebags here."

"You'll leave them both," Clint said. "Lucky the Organ Pipe sheriff is here to take them back to the bank. You, you're going to jail. Let's go."

When the four men were safely in a cell, Sheriff Patterson took a look inside the saddlebags.

"Ain't all of it, but it's a lot," he said.

"Might find some of it wherever Fellows lived," Clint said. "You can take it all back with you."

"Bank might have a reward available."

"I'll leave you an account number," Clint said. "You can wire it to me."

"You trust me?"

"Sure, why not?"

Clint headed for the door.

"Leavin' town?"

"Just as soon as I can."

"Ever find out who scrawled that message on that scrap of newspaper?"

"Nope," Clint said. "Might've been Joe Hickey, for all I know, but it's not important. It got me here, but I know one thing."

"What's that?"

"I'm not grabbing for any more scraps of paper that are blowing on the wind."

Watch for

CROSSING THE LINE

335th novel in the exciting GUNSMITH series
from Jove

Coming in November!

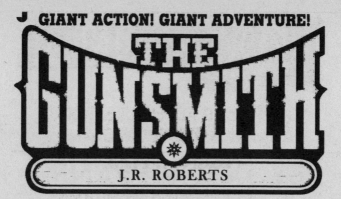

GIANT ACTION! GIANT ADVENTURE!

THE GUNSMITH

J.R. ROBERTS

Little Sureshot And
The Wild West Show
(Gunsmith Giant #9)

Dead Weight
(Gunsmith Giant #10)

Red Mountain
(Gunsmith Giant #11)

The Knights of Misery
(Gunsmith Giant #12)

The Marshal from Paris
(Gunsmith Giant #13)

Lincoln's Revenge
(Gunsmith Giant #14)

GIANT-SIZED ADVENTURE FROM
AVENGING ANGEL LONGARM.

BY TABOR EVANS

penguin.com/actionwesterns

M456AS0409

DON'T MISS A YEAR OF

Slocum Giant
by
Jake Logan

Slocum Giant 2004:
Slocum in the Secret Service

Slocum Giant 2005:
Slocum and the Larcenous Lady

Slocum Giant 2006:
Slocum and the Hanging Horse

Slocum Giant 2007:
Slocum and the Celestial Bones

Slocum Giant 2008:
Slocum and the Town Killers

Slocum Giant 2009:
Slocum's Great Race

M457AS0409